SPIN THE BOTTLE

BY DAJAN TAFARI

This is a work of fiction. All characters, events, and locations portrayed within are fictitious.

SPIN THE BOTTLE

Published by Bewere Books
Flagstaff, Arizona
https://www.bewere.us

ISBN 978-0-9995916-3-5
Printed in the United States of America
First trade paperback edition: August 2020

Cover art by Nommz

This book is dedicated to my loving boyfriend, who came into my life as if by chance and made it better every step of the way.

PART 1

Gamma Upsilon Tau was notorious on campus for having the most rigorous initiation, but I liked a challenge. Having just finished working out at the Gainsville U fitness center at the farthest edge of campus, Tailor and I stood outside the infamous frat house. We were two sweaty Cats with rank towels draped over our shoulders while chilly autumn wind ruffled the fur on our heads, arms, legs, and tails: basically everything that wasn't covered by our athletic shorts and sweat-drenched T-shirts. Sweatpants and hoodie weather was just around the corner, and Tailor was already shivering.

"Chance?" he asked with an upward prick of his ears. He was wondering why I'd stopped. My arm muscles were aching, but endorphins from the workout were pumping me up so much that I felt immune to the Midwestern winds. My tail lashed back and forth in anticipation, eyes fixed on the large brass symbols over the frat house double-doors. 'ΓΥΤ' gleamed with streaks from the October morning sun spiking through the usual dense overcast. Above the landing, red and orange maple leaves dusted the dark shingled roof. Every curtain of every window on the two-story brick building was drawn closed. The doors only ever opened for parties, and Gamma Upsilon Tau's were the biggest and best on campus.

"I'm gonna go tonight," I declared to my roommate.

Tailor rolled his eyes. "Yeah, okay. Like they're really gonna let a freshman like you in."

"Frat parties have no barrier for entry."

"Technically no, but do you really think a skinny kitty like you is gonna last among the likes of them? They're gonna eat you alive. Probably literally. I've heard the frat parties get really rowdy, especially at Gamma Upsilon Tau. You put enough drunk Furs in a room together with that kind of high-octane masculinity, *someone* is going to be eaten. You wouldn't catch me dead at one of those parties."

"I think you're being a bit unfair. *Lots* of students indulge in Predation." Chance spent his pre-orientation weeks mentally preparing himself for a higher sense of awareness. On a college campus like this one, Predation could happen anywhere at any time. Crossing his arms behind his head, Chance argued, "You're no safer in a lecture hall than a frat house."

"That's just objectively not true. It's literally in our student handbook: No Predation in the classrooms, library, or any place that would disrupt the learning environment."

"Yes yes, I'm sure you know *all* the rules verbatim," I groaned throwing my paws in the air. Tailor could be real annoying like that. In fairness, he was right. The campus liked to treat Predation like making out, and when I stopped to think about it, the comparison wasn't *that* far off. The RAs told us at orientation that if you wouldn't make out in a library or a computer lab or a classroom or a bathroom—yada yada—don't gulp someone there. If you're going to eat a peer, don't be indecent about it. Most Furs were considerate enough to keep that behavior confined to their dorm rooms; though it wasn't unusual to see someone walking around with a squirming belly. That said, most professors added a rule to their syllabus to time your digestion so that it finishes *before* class. Sounds of struggles and pleadings to be let out had a tendency to interrupt lectures unless the predator's belly was fat enough to muffle *all* sound.

Needless to say, frat houses could be, and often were, a sort of predatory free-for all. It was part of what allegedly made the parties so exciting. "Anyways, I've made it *this* long without being gulped. I think I could handle the Gamma Upsilon Taus."

Turning away from me, Tailor started back down the leaf-strewn sidewalk toward the mess hall. "Yeah keep holding onto that mindset. I'll give whatever belly you end up in a smack when you're proven wrong."

I jogged to catch up with him. "Hey! I ain't no one's prey."

Tailor shoved his paws in the pockets of his nylon shorts. His muzzle was curled up in a confident smirk. The Siamese Cat was taller than me by a couple of inches, and when he cast a sideways glance down at me, his pupils were slits. "It's only midterms. Give it time."

I flexed my arms for him, swelling my biceps through my thick orange fur. He may have had height on me, but as a Tabby Cat, I was stockier, stronger. My arms and pecs befitted my height, and if I stuck to my current regimen, my abs would start showing through my stomach fur within a few more weeks. Height advantage or no, I could easily take Tailor in a fight. To prove it, I playfully shouldered him off the sidewalk. He laughed and came back at me, and our paws were locked in each others'. We faced each other, twisting around on the sidewalk. Palm to palm, fingers interwoven, and muscles lumped in active use, we wrestled upright, arms locked at right angles while trying to gain ground on each other. Tailor sneered and showed his little fangs.

"Come at me, ya Siamese twink," I goaded. His white fur, punctuated with bold chocolate on his ear tips, nose, and paws, was soft and silky, and because it was so short, his physique was easy to poke fun at. "The only reason *you* haven't been eaten yet, is cuz you're all skin and bones."

Tailor waggled his eyes. The light green orbs were expressive, and no amount of feline coyness could ever mask his mood. He was so gay he couldn't even keep a straight face. My teasing broke him into blushing, and that was when I gained the upper paw. Sidestepping behind him, I wrapped my arms around his slender stomach and lifted him off the ground. "Ha! I gotcha!"

"I let you have me," he teased.

I dropped him and shouldered past him back on the way to the student union up ahead. "Yeah sure."

"I just wanted to be in those strong, strong arms." I knew he was being sarcastic; we had only both begun our weight training a couple weeks ago, and so far I was more or less coasting on the natural muscle genetics had gifted me. Even for my species, I was a tad on the short side, but if I could heft someone my own size, then that was something I could boast. I would only get stronger. I was determined.

We got a quick early lunch: chicken and veggie wraps. We were trying to eat healthy, and the Gainsville mess hall's breakfast options were more catered to those destined to *gain* their freshman fifteen. We decided to eat on the go; the cafeteria could get really rowdy on Saturday mornings. As we waited in line to pay for our food, we spotted a crowd of jocks having just finished with an early football practice. Mostly traditional predator species, they greatly outsized us. Bears, Tigers, Lions, and other big cats. The only leaf-munchers were a Stag and a Moose. Girls crowded around them in fawning clusters. Some were literal Fawns batting their freshman Doe eyes. With my wrap in paw, I elbowed Tailor on the way out. "Just watch. By the time I'm a junior, I'll be an upperclassman member of Gamma Upsilon Tau and on one of the varsity teams."

Tailor noted the Bear lineman. He was pretty portly with a belly that barely fit into his jersey. "You'll be on a varsity *some*thing."

Everyone knew that the varsity team ate freshmen the week before each home game. Allegedly, a good lean Anthro was good for calorie packing and testosterone. The coaches often gave tips on the sort of people to target on their hunts. I looked Tailor up and down. "You're more their type than me. And you're a lot more likely to get lured into their maws." We were almost to the mess hall door and well away from their cluster, so I didn't mind talking about them now. There were a lot of active preds on campus, but it was best to let them be open about their practices rather than assume. Sometimes Furs were just naturally fat and took offense to the insinuation they'd recently eaten someone whole. It was best to avoid those kinds of faux pas (especially around people much larger than you).

"What's that supposed to mean?" Tailor demanded behind me.

I opened the door to crisp fall air and inhaled it deeply. Now it was my turn to feel cocky. "You're telling me that if one of those big cats beckoned their finger at you, you wouldn't hop right into their lap?"

Our dorms were just on the other end of campus, with the student union plopped right between them. Tailor rounded me. Walking backwards like a campus tour guide, he narrowed his eyes and pointed a finger at me. "No, and let me tell you why. It's cuz I know a pred when I see one, and I'm not stupid. You know I came from a town with a ridiculously high Predation rate. In this world there are two things that keep you safe from being someone's meal: being an active predator yourself and being smart. You're neither." Tailor turned around and started marching ahead. He folded his paws behind his back and stuck his snout in the air. "I have the smarts though."

I stopped and wrinkled my muzzle. "I'm smart."

Tailor glanced over his shoulder. "Tell that to your midterm scores. Maybe *they're* dumb enough to believe you."

I jogged up to him to match his pace. I wanted to be mad, but I razzed him for a lot of things. Being gay, skinny and frail, and really goddamn pretentious with his music choices. *Hip-hop about butts could be just as artistic as Mozart, you fucking nerd.* But just because he was acing his way to an engineering degree, and I had near straight C's and still hadn't declared a major, didn't mean I was dumb. I just hadn't decided what I wanted yet.

"I could be a pred," I argued instead. That would be an easier argument to win against the brainiac. The Siamese Cat laughed.

"I could!"

He laughed harder, and hunching my shoulders, I grumbled to myself the rest of the way back.

The dorm room we shared was a testament to our differing personalities. While we weren't the type of roommates that felt the need to establish "sides of the room," sides developed on their own over the course of the semester. Tailor's side was organized and neat, and my side was... well... practical. I often thought it pointless to "put away" that which I used every day. This same philosophy applied to making the bed and the sloppy pile of toiletries I kept on the counter. Meanwhile, Tailor arranged his textbooks on the shelf above his desk by size; he sorted his Gatorade under his bed by color–forming a rainbow—which I teased him about but also found a bit quaint; and one time when he wasn't in the room I tried to bounce a quarter off his neatly taut bedspread, and it actually fucking rebounded.

Tailor plopped down at his desk chair as soon as we entered our dorm. He wanted to get a head start on his homework due Monday. I was content to take my time. I swiped the stack of folders and papers off my desk and onto my bed, loaded some YouTube videos, and unwrapped my meal from its foil. I was about to take the first bite, but then I paused. I glanced over my shoulder to check on Tailor. He already had an Excel sheet open, rapidly tapping in calculations for some lab report of his.

While he was engrossed in his work, I opened my mouth as wide as I could. Forming a large O with my muzzle, I stuck out my tongue and nudged the thick wrap into my jaws. Eyes squinted shut, I felt the whole thing slide in, but it only got a few inches up my sandpapery tongue before the hinge of my jaws started to ache from hyperextension. They were barely wide enough for the overly stuffed tortilla.

I tried to imagine how predators managed to fit entire heads in here, let alone shoulders and beyond. Most predators could swallow anyone their size and smaller. Really good ones could even go a bit larger, though that was rare. With a short gagging sound, I pulled the wrap out; a strand of drool oozed down my chin. I wiped it on my arm and looked at the wrap again. Just swallowing this in one gulp was intimidating. Massaging my mandible, I wondered if this was what lock jaw felt like. I tried again, and got it a bit farther in, but then it brushed against my uvula, and it all went south.

My stomach clenched with the force of a vice. I lurched forward and coughed hard. The wrap plopped back into my open paws and tore open a bit from the impact. After hacking for a few moments, I managed to suppress the urge to vomit. Already anticipating a weird look, I glanced over my shoulder. On the other side of the room, Tailor was leaning back in his chair, arm draped over the back of it. He bore a smug grin. "You know," he said with a smirk, "if you really wanna know what deep-throating feels like, you're welcome to try on me."

Through fits of coughs, I managed a strained, "Fuck you."

"What are you doing?"

I tossed the wrap on the unfolded square of foil on my desk and crossed my arms. "I'm not used to swallowing things."

"I am."

I rolled my eyes. "Bitch, I'm serious."

"Are you upset about what I said about you predding?"

My muzzle twitched, and I looked askance. "No."

"You've gotta be the most prideful Cat I've ever met, and I grew up with my baby boomer grandparents." Except for times when he brought it up, I often forgot Tailor's parents were both eaten when he and his brothers were cubs. "You know there are worse things to be bad at," he said. "Not everyone can do it."

"I want to though."

"Since when?" Tailor spread his arms in bafflement. "You've *never* mentioned this before."

Miffed, my whiskers twitched. My ear flicked. "I've always wanted to be a pred," I lied. In reality it was never one of my interests. I wanted a flat, muscled bod, and eating other Anthros whole made that very difficult to maintain. But it had always been *my* choice not to eat other people. What pissed me off was Tailor telling me I couldn't. I could do anything I set my mind to.

The only reason my grades sucked was because I didn't care. C's get degrees, and I didn't want to waste the best years of my life with my snout buried in books. I wanted it buried in pussy. This was my time to live it up before, as my dad put it, 'The world starts its daily dump on you.'

Tailor rolled his eyes and turned his attention back to his monitor. "Chance, just eat your damn wrap like a normal Fur." Then after a pause he added, "And do your homework."

Ignoring his mom-like nagging about homework, I argued, "I don't wanna eat like a 'normal' Fur."

College was my one shot to truly experiment and try new things. This time-tested opportunity could let me prove I was more than a tiny Tabby twerp. For lack of a better word, it was my *chance* to be more than the shrimpy son of a dumbass divorced fisherman.

Tailor snorted. "You were that kid who licked the frozen flag pole in winter on a dare, weren't you?"

"No." I was the one who punched Jeremy Philly in the snout when he called me fat. I was the one who broke an arm on the bike ramp made of garbage when everyone else pussied out. I was the one who looked my homeroom teacher in the eye and spat in her stupid Pug face when she said my grades were too low for college, and the detention be damned. Anyone could be a pred in this world. Even Hamsters could do it if they could get their chubby cheeks over someone's head. Biology and species had nothing to do with it. Just size. I may have been only five and a half feet tall, but so were a lot of Anthros. "I want a fuckin' shower," I grumbled. "Not everyone's trying to attract every horny guy on campus with musk."

Tailor chomped on his lip. "Wow." He steepled his fingers and inhaled. "I'm gonna let that one slide, because clearly I've pissed you off, but that one was over the line."

He was right. There was light teasing—he teased me whenever I got caught staring at a chick's boobs—but even I could acknowledge that was playing too much into stereotypes. I should've apologized, but instead I just stalked across the

room and threw my wrap in his lap. "Have fun being 'normal.'"
I scooped my shower shit into a bag, grabbed my towel off the
hook by the door, and without looking at my roommate, growled,
"I'm going to that frat party tonight. I'm going hungry, and I'm
coming home with a full stomach."

Out of the corner of my eye, I caught Tailor staring with a
slack jaw. There was a mixture of disgust and irritation in those
big green eyes. But fuck what he thought about it.

I felt a little better after my shower. Secluded in my own tiled
cell where I could let everything hang out, I washed the anger
down the drain with the sweat and dirt from my workout. The
curtain screeched on old metal when I yanked it open. With a
towel wrapped around my waist, I stepped into the communal
changing area where my clothes waited on a varnished wooden
bench against the wall. For a freshman dorm, the bathrooms
were well maintained. All that private school tuition was at least
coming back to us in some way.

The changing section led out to the main area of the
communal bathroom where low sinks and broad stalls that
could accommodate most species with ease were separated by
a wide expanse of more tile floor. It was mostly empty save for a
Red Fox, also donning only a towel, who was trimming his cheek
ruffs with a pair of snipping scissors. I'd occasionally seen him
around the dorm before. He was narrow in his hips but broad
in shoulders, and while he wasn't ripped, his body shape gave
him an enviable swimmer's build, and his arms possessed fair
definition. I'd seen Tailor checking him out, and even I could
admit there was some appeal there. The Red had the flat stomach
of a non-active predator, which I was sure also caught Tailor's
interest. If my roommate even suspected someone on the floor
was a predator, he kept his distance. He was so paranoid like
that.

Large mirrors behind the sinks reflected both of us as I sidled
up next to the Red Fox (while obviously keeping a respectable
no-homo distance). Of course he was taller than me, almost six

and a half feet, maybe more. Subtly glancing at his musculature, I wondered if, like with his height, he was just lucky with genetics or if he had some workout tips he could share that would carve that sort of shapeliness onto my own torso. I knew that bulking up only went so far to appease the frustration of vertically challenged folks like myself, but-

He cast yellow eyes on me. Fuck, I'd been staring.

"What brand of scissors are those?" I stammered to save face. "Mine keep breaking."

The Fox turned the scissors in his paws and angled the little black 'M' logo at me without saying anything. I didn't recognize it, but I wasn't actually interested. I was just desperate to not be labeled a queer my first semester. That shit stuck, and the last thing I wanted was an unshakable rainbow reputation of undateability spread among the ladies.

Though now that I thought about it, maybe a bit of a trim around my chubby Tabby cheeks could make my face look leaner. The rest of me would take more effort, but a ruff trim could be a decent start. I stroked my stomach, appraising the reflection of its slight solid curve. If I probed deep, I could feel the muscles cocooned beneath the beergut that blossomed from my under-aged drinking habits. I could only imagine how much I would probably balloon out if I actually *did* try Predation. I'd look like a goddamn miniature sumo.

Maybe I could swallow someone and let them out after showing off the full stomach, I mulled over. Then I could have it both ways. I could prove I was more than a diminutive Cat and save the future abs I'd been cultivating. If I snapped a few pics of a squirming belly, I'd have something I could lord over Tailor's head for the rest of the year. Then next time he rubbed his grades in my face I could be like, "Yeah, well I fuckin' *ate* someone. Top that, beeyotch." That would certainly shut up that stuck-up twink.

I grabbed one of the pawheld furdryers off the wall fixture and flipped it on. The drone and screech of the machine blocked out all other sounds in the bathroom as hot air blasted my chest.

I was dripping from the shower, but after a couple of minutes my orange fur started fluffing up again. Thick fur was the worst. It took forever to dry and it hid musculature ruthlessly. It was only under the deluge of steaming air moving my fur around at its roots that really showed off just how prominent my pecs were for someone of my stature.

Of course, with the furdryer going, it also revealed the subtle dome of my stomach. The mirror put it on display, and discomfort itched through all my muscles. I didn't want to be represented with a body like this. Wincing, I sucked in my gut. Just being next to the Fox, who towered over me by a foot or more and still was thinner, made me self-conscious. Fuck beer. If my dad wasn't such a cheap-ass I could've been sneaking vodka like every other high school senior. Then maybe the paunch of baby fat I'd been whittling down since junior high wouldn't have hardened into this gross precursory gut. I let it drop and squeezed it gently. My stomach only bowled out an inch or so past my crotch at the convexity of a dinner plate, but I hated the way it all retained a uniform rigidity like stretched trampoline mesh.

The Red Fox sized me up again with those yellow eyes, sour as lemons. His black muzzle twisted in a cocky sneer. I wanted to punch him; that was how we solved things in my old neighborhood. But the student guidebook preached that I had to be less hot-headed. The vulpine returned his focus to himself. He set the scissors at the edge of his sink with a light tap of metal on granite and with long black fingers gripped his own chin. He twisted his face this way and that, scrunching and smiling. Appreciating the symmetry of his grooming, he went to the showers.

His tail snaked up out of the towel and swayed back and forth with a rhythm opposite his hips as he walked, and I couldn't tell if that sassy motion was emblemizing behaviors meant to look stereotypically gay or stereotypically Fox. Just before he leaned into the center shower stall with the curtain still open, he dropped his towel. He cast a sneer over his shoulder before tossing the towel over the shower curtain. As I replayed that whole interaction in my head, I realized that what I thought was douchey scorn from him being so much more fit than me now registered that he might have thought I *was* checking him out and his leer was just a derisive rejection for a pursuit I wasn't even interested in. Ugh, I hated Foxes.

"Damn, I love Foxes," a gruff voice rumbled next to me.

I glanced to my right. A hefty shirtless Boar with a huge furry belly sagging past the waistband of his sweatpants stared with rapt attention at the Fox. The furdryer was still running, and I hadn't heard the clops of his hooves sneak up on me. I almost fell over from the surprise. Caught off guard, I coughed and caught my footing while putting a comfortable buffer of space between us. The huge porker had been practically brushing against me with his crossed arms and love handles.

Not bothering with any semblance of modesty, the Red Fox twisted the water knob to "hot" with a hiss. Back turned to us, he held his paw under the deluge as mist rose up around him. His tail continued to sway even after he'd stalled his hips.

"Just fucking look at that," the Boar crooned. He snorted through his tusks and licked his lips.

I was gonna blurt out something like, "I prefer girls" so that he didn't get the wrong idea, but I also didn't wanna be one of *those* guys so insecure that he had to say how great boobs were every time a gay guy opened their mouth. So instead I just nodded. "Would be nice to have," I admitted. It wasn't a lie, since I *had* been staring just as much as this horny Boar. I just would have rather had a body like that for myself rather than under me... or Heaven forbid on top of me. I shuddered.

"I call dibs," the Boar grunted with a wink.

I stepped back. "Oh by all means. I prefer girls." I still felt douchey, but at least now we were making conversation so it didn't feel as heteronormatively unsolicited as it would have eight seconds ago.

The Boar nodded and clapped me on the shoulders. "Oh yeah, I like girls too."

"You're bi?" I didn't like asking people about their sexuality—it was none of my business who someone fucked—but it didn't seem *in*appropriate for the topic.

Movement and a screech snagged my attention from the Boar. The Red Fox had stepped under the water and shut the curtain, and as if confident that the curtain would block sound, the Boar spoke louder. He gripped the towel draped over his shoulder by the ends. He laughed, and his big belly shook. "Oh naw naw. Straight all the way." Then he bent over and leaned in close, tongue slapping his thick chops. "But between you and me, guys just taste better. More meat on 'em. 'Scuse me."

My eyes widened. I shouldn't have been surprised given the Boar's bulk. Before I could say anything else, the Boar pushed past me and clopped into the shower area. Without even a second's hesitation, he tossed his towel off to the side with a flick, and rammed his bulk through the curtain.

"Gah! What the hel-" came the Fox's voice over the stream of water on tile, but it was quickly muffled with deep slurping sounds.

They both barely fit in the stall. The Boar's broad rotund hindquarters and the small of his back swelled out the white curtain like an overweight ghost. The surrounding edges of the curtain flapped with a flailing of limbs.

I looked around the bathroom. Was anyone else watching? This was risky as hell. The bathrooms were the only place in the dorms where Predation wasn't allowed. Lots of arguments were made against that: sanitation, privacy, etc. It was also a little tacky to jump a prey when they were naked and vulnerable. This was very much against the rules. I mean... I was the one who not a half hour ago told Tailor that predding could happen anywhere, but in one of the few banned spaces with a witness was brazen as fuck. This Hog was either stupid or really confident, and in my own experiences, you didn't get a pred belly that big by being stupid.

A flash of movement caught my eye in the narrow gap between curtain rod and the ceiling. Black vulpine foot paws flipped up into the air, kicking and twitching as they steadily dropped back down out of view. The Boar's grunts of wrangling and exertion could be heard over the spray of the shower, as could his hearty gulps. Finally the movement and sounds from within the stall ceased. The shower turned off.

Fat umber fingers curled around the curtain and screeched it open. The Boar stood where there was once a lithe muscular Fox. With sweatpants drenched dark gray and water dripping over the curves of his huge body, he leaned back against the tiled wall and licked his lips. His eyes were crossed in ecstasy. His belly had almost doubled in size and wobbled on his wide hips. Enough fat hung on the Boar's body that the lumps of the prey weren't too pronounced like I'd seen on other stuffed stomachs. Only faint swells rose and fell on the front and sides of his gut as his prey struggled inside of him. Sometimes you could hear the prey's muffled cries from inside their fleshy prisons. This predator was too fat for that, even in this echoey room.

The Boar covered his mouth with his fist and belched. It was loud and wet, and it echoed off the tiled walls with such resonance that, were my eyes closed, I could have convinced myself that *I* was the one in the belly with the way it rebounded off every wall.

"Mmm, fuck that was good," he moaned. He patted his belly, talking to no one in particular, but then he seemed to recall that I was here, and his eyes narrowed on me. "Anyone gonna find out about this?" It was as much a threat as a challenge, and it was one that even I wasn't willing to take. I shook my head, and the Boar chuckled. He walked out of view and plopped down on the changing bench. I heard the *plap* of wet fat on wet wood. Cat curiosity lured me back into the shower room. It wasn't like I'd never seen a full pred belly. It wasn't uncommon to see a stuffed predator hobble across the quad now and then. And yet, as I stood in this humid room with shower mist hovering across the cold floor like graveyard fog, all I could do was stare at this fellow freshman's enormous belly.

Up until a few moments ago, I was envying that Fox's strong

frame, wishing I could have that level of confidence with myself, thinking that if only I was a bit bigger and stronger, then I could hold my own in this eat-or-be-eaten world, but this Boar just gobbled him up like it was nothing. I knew size and strength mattered, but this Boar was in a whole other league entirely. Two confident Furs were in this room though, and the one who I had wanted to look like, even *be* like, was now stewing in an enormous stomach. By tomorrow he'd be a layer of fat on this big guy's body, blended with God knows how many had been gulped down before him. But this pred... *he* had confidence too. He was confident enough to eat a fellow student where he wasn't supposed to and confident enough to buy my silence with just a few words and a look, and when I thought about it, *that* was what I *really* wanted. I wanted that kind of confidence and respect. What was the point of muscles if they didn't help in any way in overpowering a huge predator like this guy? Especially if muscle just made me look more appetizing to preds, as the Boar put it.

He loosened the drawstrings on his sopping sweatpants and wormed them down to his ankles with difficulty. Once he'd kicked them to the wet floor with a *slap*, he covered himself with his towel. "Do me a favor?" he asked. "Plop these in the dryer? I'll slip you some quarters the next time I bump into you." He slapped his gut.

Now his voice was devoid of any threat. He wasn't talking to me as a predator, but just as a fellow freshman wanting to bum laundry machine money. "Uhh... sure." How do you say 'no' to such a simple request? After all, we were floormates before he ate that Fox, and he would be a floormate long after the Fox was gurgled.

"Thanks, man. I'm gonna occupy the big stall until this guy settles down." At the end of the room, the most spacious shower stall had a bench for disabled Furs as well as enormous Elephants and Hippos who had a hard time standing for long periods of time. "I'd hate to bump into the RA on my way back to my room. I saw him on the way here, and if he saw me now he'd know I was hunting where it's off limits."

I chuckled. "Yeah, and it's not like you could just eat him."

"Oh I definitely could," he boasted. Hefting his gut with both arms, he wobbled the enormous mass of fat up and down. The prey inside thrashed, and the lumps translating across the expanse of dark brown fur showed just how much space the Fox was filling up. I eyed the Boar skeptically, and he smirked. "The RA's not *that* big."

"I suppose. Though if you ate the RA, then you'd *really* be in trouble."

"Only if someone tattles," he said waggling his eyebrows at me suggestively. *Technically*, RAs were "off the menu" when it came to campus-wide Predation rules, like faculty and staff. The problem was, RAs were a lot harder to pick out of a crowd than an old grey-muzzle professor. It was mostly a policy to make sure students in dorms didn't just eat the RAs to cover up other rule breaking, but unless an RA had enough clout to be recognized all across campus, they were really only safe in their dorm buildings. No one could be expected to keep track of all the RAs on campus, so of course, RAs went missing now and then. It couldn't be helped, and unless the school could conclusively prove an RA was eaten by one of their own residents, nothing was done. That would require a *very* brave witness of course. College is supposed to prepare you for real life. In real life, no one was 'off the menu.' Rules like this kept things running smoother in controlled environments, but in the real world, anyone could be made a meal of at any time.

The very fact that this Boar was right here, currently housing one of our own in his gargantuan gut, was proof of that. I thought about how easily the big guy had snuck up on me. What if he'd had a taste for a Cat instead of a Fox? I'd be the one inside of his stomach, and there wouldn't have been anything I could do about it. It was a testament to how small and weak I really was, and thinking about that made me almost want to concede that Tailor had a point. It was *not* a concession I wanted to make.

Between pinched fingers, I gathered up the sopping sweats,

a whopping sixty inches around the waist—damn—and took care of the favor asked of me, while the Boar hefted himself onto his hooves and stepped back behind a curtain. Holding the pants away from my recently dried fur, I scampered out of the bathroom, carrying with me a new dip in my own confidence.

I ducked into the room for quarters without sparing a glance at Tailor and went to dump the soggy pants. When I got back though, I found my wrap was back on my desk, rerolled and neat (despite the slight tear in the side from my earlier rough treatment). Tailor was still at his desk, hunkered forward with eyes on his excel sheet.

I dropped my towel and got dressed. He never looked at me; though, I wouldn't have cared if he did. I told him so after our first week together when he told me he was gay. Real men dropped their pants in front of each other all the time. I already endured six years of it in P.E. I wasn't going to treat him differently and, jokes I made against him aside, I wasn't about to act like one of those dude-bro homophobes.

I assured myself that, despite my teasing, I was really tolerant, especially compared to most Furs. After all, if I lived with a girl I'd sure as hell steal as many glances as I could. Obviously I don't want folks on campus thinking *I'm* gay, but Tailor choosing to check me out wasn't going to affect that.

I chose to be lazy with how languidly I pulled my pants up today, actually hoping he would notice and remember I don't actually have any problem with his sexuality, but he either didn't notice or wouldn't take the bait. So once dressed, I stood in the center of the room, in jeans and a T-shirt that featured a band I liked. I puffed out my cheeks in a sigh, hoping he would say... anything really. I wanted to imagine his tight frown was just concentration, but I knew he was still upset at me. *Just apologize*, you dumb fuck, but *I* was still mad at what he'd said against *me*.

"Thanks for fixing my wrap," I finally said. It was the best I could force out.

No response.

"Seriously. You take it. You like 'em more."

Again the Siamese Cat said nothing. I grabbed the wrap off my desk and held it out to him, wishing he would close the other half of the distance and take it or at least look at me. Then my roommate yanked open his desk drawer and pulled out a pair of earbuds. He crammed the nubs deep into his fan-like ears and hooked them up to his laptop.

Rolling my eyes, I tossed the wrap in the garbage and plopped down at my own desk with a disgruntled huff.

As the afternoon idled away, I couldn't shake what I'd witnessed in the bathroom. I wondered if that Boar was still in the shower stall. When it came to digestion, a lot of variables could affect the amount of time it took: the size of the prey, the size of the pred, the pred's metabolism, and how much of a fight the prey were able to put up before blacking out. According to what some of my old high school friends said, it could take anywhere between six to twelve hours to gurgle someone up. I imagined that unless the Boar was the sort to go out of his way to keep his prey alive and kicking as long as possible, the Red Fox would have had to have at *least* passed out by now and allow the Boar to make an innocuous enough walk back to his dorm.

I decided not to say anything about it to Tailor—even if we *had* been talking to each other. He'd probably wanna snitch on the guy. 'But eating people in the bathroom is against the rules,' he'd say. He could be a real pain about that kind of stuff. Plus I was sure that the Boar meant it when he implied that he'd eat me if he got in trouble for shower-snacking. I knew there was always a risk of being gobbled up by someone every time I went out, but why take unnecessary risks? I had better things to occupy myself with. Like the party tonight. Tailor would surely say *that* is also an unnecessary risk, but fuck it. If I can't indulge in a few contradictions when I'm nineteen, when could I?

Tailor was being stubbornly quiet and I just wanted to get out of this tense silence and dull my senses with noise and vodka.

A part of me wished I'd gone to more of those bullshit socials at the beginning of the semester so that I knew more people around the floor. Hell, I didn't even know that Boar's *or* that Fox's name. It would suck to go to the party alone. *I'm sure I'll meet some people there*, I figured. I wasn't gonna be one of those assholes who just get hosed and keep to themselves all night. It would be nice to have a group to show up with, though. Sometimes I really missed high school. Everyone that went there was a low-brow dick, but at least they were dicks that I knew. How did anyone meet new people outside of ragers? Did they just go to cafés and talk to people? What kind of fuckery was that?

I slumped in my chair and browsed Furrynook for a bit. I had over two hundred "friends" from high school, but so many of the chicks had married right after graduation that I didn't recognize a lot of their new names. I only closely followed a few people.

James, a Wolverine, had finally gotten a job as a garbage man, and his new profile pic depicted him with a big gut. Guess he took up predding on his routes. I couldn't blame him. Every day on the job was probably like going through a drive-thru. Carlos, this stoner Blue Jay I occasionally smoked with at parties, was going to community college. He was still enrolled after ten weeks, which meant I owed my boy Stank twenty bucks. I was surprised the loudmouth Skunk hadn't started hounding me already for me to pay up, and so I thought I might check up on him. When I typed his name into the search bar nothing came up.

Weird, I acknowledged clearing out the bar. I wondered if he'd nixed his old nickname. It would make sense. A Skunk going by the name Stank was pretty juvenile. Instead I typed in his real name, but that didn't churn up any results either. I knew folks didn't use Furrynook as much as they used to, but I found it odd that Stank would have shut down his profile. Last I heard he was working the graveyard shift at the dingy convenience store that used to sell us beer that was a day past sell-date. We used to go there a couple times a month because the manager said he'd rather risk the fine of selling to a minor than dump perfectly good merch. Working at a shit hole like that wouldn't exactly compel someone to close a Furrynook account. I could have easily just texted him, but I was already invested in the thrill of a social media mystery so I tried one last thing: I typed in his email address that he mostly used for porn subscriptions and got a hit.

My eyes widened. No wonder I hadn't found him. He hadn't changed his name. Someone else did. Where once was a picture of Stank in a beanie and two middle fingers bookending his cheek ruffs, now featured a close-up of an exposed Tiger belly. I could see the faint black points of stripe wraparounds fading into cream-colored fur. Twin sags bound in the bunched-up hem of a T-shirt filled the upper corners: a pair of big tits displaced by the rotundity of the gut. Instead of Stank's name, the profile was headlined: "Kara's Belly Fat."

I leaned back in my chair and huffed in disbelief. Stank got himself eaten by some Tiger chick? I tried to think of the Tigers we went to high school with. There hadn't been a lot. Kara didn't ring a bell. I mean... he was always going out with people I'd never heard of from out of town. I assumed this Kara had to be one of those people if she'd managed to get into his account like this. Finders keepers was common practice among preds, but they had to have known each other pretty well for him to fork over his phone password.

I scrolled down a bit more to see if I could glean any other information about this feline, but she was pretty sparse with her posts. She'd only updated his status three times:

"Looking for your Skunk friend? Post any last things you wanna tell him below. I'll pass it on before he becomes Tig fat."

"Nearly done gurgling. *Burrrrp*"

"Oof. That was good. I'm still hungry if any of you guys wanna join him. Send me a message. We'll meet in the middle and then I'll send you to MY middle lol."

That last post garnered a collection of angry emojis and choice language. Seeing as the party had come and gone already, I didn't bother checking out the replies to the previous two.

I couldn't believe I'd missed this. I guess college had kept me busier than I thought. If I had to guess, I'd say more than half his connections had already unfriended his ghosted account. I remember seeing some stats article once that said that in the next 30 years there would be more profiles for people who'd been eaten than people who weren't.

Not seeing much of a point to keeping this unknown Tiger belly in my friends list, I clicked the "unfriend" button looming at the top of the page. Best to move on quickly. It was weird I supposed. I knew the guy for eight or nine years, and I wasn't even upset. This kinda shit happened on the daily where I was from so it was pretty easy to shrug off. It wasn't like I had big plans to maintain contact with everyone from my old shitty high school. That Tiger girl did what the passage of time would have done eventually. "Time digests all of us," as the big-brain philosophers say. I minimized the tab and internally celebrated the macabre reason for saving twenty bucks before vowing to pour one out tonight for the former cashier.

I snorted to myself. Maybe it would be more appropriate to pour a drink out for the big feline who was able to stomach a Skunk. Stank used to tease me all the time that I was more likely to get eaten before him; he was always so confident that no one would eat a stinky guy like him. But in this crazy world, not even a Fart Squirrel like him was safe, and he regularly stunk worse than Carlos after a whole night of puffing. And here Tailor thinks that "smarts" is all you need.

Granted, Stank wasn't the brightest bulb in the chandelier, I highly doubted a few more IQ points would have made a difference on a pred as determined as that Tiger. I glanced over my shoulder where the skinny Siamese Cat tapped away at his laptop like the little nerd he was. Our duo weekend workouts wouldn't cut it in this world, maybe not even on this campus. What could some meager muscles on a Cat do to ward off preds that a rank Skunk spray couldn't?

It made me feel small and weak to think about. Flexing my arms, the last few weeks of progress didn't seem like as much as they had this morning. Tailor's lack of confidence in me gnawed away at me. There was no way in hell I'd end up like Stank. For starters, I wouldn't date big fucking predator girls—I still felt convinced that had been the connection based on my earlier deductions. Second, I wouldn't make the mistake that that Red Fox did, which is being all muscly and appetizing to preds like that big hungry Boar. If I was gonna make it with the big boys, I was going to have to become one of the big boys, and I only felt more sure of my original wants for tonight. I would go to that frat party, and I would nab my first ever prey. A ΓΥΤ party would be the perfect place to test the waters of Predation. A wild party like that would be sink or swim, and that's how I fuckin' liked it.

I spent the next couple hours on predator forums in search of tips for first-time swallowers. A lot of it was useless drivel. 'Practice makes perfect.' 'Just relax.' Fuck that shit. I needed *actual* guidance. If you wanna learn how to be good at football, you don't need the nonsense on fuckin' motivational posters. You need to know what to physically do: where to put your feet, how to grip a ball to your chest, where to aim for a solid tackle.

Unfortunately, it was hard to actually find helpful stuff. Predation was treated like sex when it came to the Internet. If you wanted to know what to actually do, you needed to get off social media and risk a computer virus. Ten pages into my Google search, I finally stumbled across a link that didn't look like it would infect my hard drive with virtual syphilis, and I struck gold: actual preds doing more than boasting about how many prey they could scarf in a month. This was the research I needed.

Apparently starving yourself *wasn't* the way to go. Now I felt doubly stupid for wasting my wrap. Most accounts on the forum confirmed it was good to indulge in a light snack an hour or so before predding to stimulate the appetite more. My stomach growled, so I decided to fetch a bag of chips from my snack shelf and then returned to my desk. I hadn't eaten anything since my granola bar breakfast, and that was before a rigorous workout.

Scanning onward, another comment really stuck out to me: 'Don't try swallowing normal food whole. It just builds up false confidence. It's the equivalent of playing a lot of Rock Band and then thinking you're good at the guitar.' With that in mind I scrolled farther down that particular thread, because I knew the swallowing process was going to be an issue for me, especially given my smaller-than-normal stature. Another great nugget of help suggested, 'Don't try to force your jaws open. It's all in the cheeks. You need to relax those if you wanna get a whole person down your throat. Obviously staying calm is key. Otherwise you clench, and you might choke, and that's just embarrassing for both parties.' A reply added, 'That said, even though your jaw's not that important for predding, be warned it might dislocate, especially on your first time. It'll hurt, but it'll be worth it. Just stay calm and pop it back into place afterwards.' So there actually was some merit to this 'staying calm' thing, but it was much more informative to tack it onto some context.

Shifting in my seat so my back was to the window, I propped my legs up on my bed. I wiggled my toes on my pillow and wondered what I would do if suddenly they were disappearing down a slippery pred gullet, into deep moist darkness. I tried to imagine watching my own body disappear beyond someone else's muzzle, and I couldn't help but shudder at the thought. Based on these tips though, it was far more likely I'd be swallowed head first. In fact most of the comments recommended swallowing your prey that way, what with most of your prospective meals being eye-level or shorter. A lot of these tips were really encouraging; they made me realize that eating someone was actually easier than I thought, but on the flip-side of course, it meant it was also easier than I thought to wind up as someone else's dinner. Granted, you always had to keep your head on swivel when out and about, but I guess I never considered how easily it could affect me.

I thought back to this morning when we had passed by the Gamma Upsilon Tau house. Some hungover frat boy could have just sauntered out and taken us both for breakfast without a second thought. I genuinely couldn't imagine a more insufferable way to go than stew away while crammed up against uptight Tailor. I shook my head, trying not to think about such an unpleasant fate. I needed to learn more if I was going to be a predator myself.

A third person chimed in on the post with, 'You can use your jaws to help clamp a really struggly prey down, but it's usually not necessary. Once they're in the throat just focus on getting them upright. Letting gravity help is totally valid. I've been eating prey for three years now, and I still use that to help get the big ones down.'

When I thought about it, I'd seen that tactic a lot. Even the big hungry Boar from the showers had presumably done that. He'd been behind the curtain so I hadn't been able to see that well, but I remembered how the Red Fox's legs had been upended into the air before sinking from view accompanied by those loud, hasty gulps. If even an experienced predator—I'm assuming he's experienced given his ample girth—did the gravity drop technique, then it was something I should consider too. I imagined overpowering prey was no simple task.

Without meaning to, I glanced at Tailor. His tail swayed back and forth through the back of his chair. His shoulders were hunched over his keyboard. He was the kind of person I'd have to target at the party tonight, someone I was equally matched with. Recalling our playful wrestling outside of the frat house earlier, I tried to reimagine it. What if one of us had tried eating the other. I wondered which of us would have won.

From looking at these forum posts, I would have wanted to do things way differently. We'd locked arms, which pitted both of our upper-body strengths against each other. Apparently, that was a bad way to go about it, especially if you were about the same size as your meal. You wanted to keep their arms down at all costs so that they couldn't push back and get away... or worse, revenge-eat you right back. I bet I could get his arms pinned to his sides if I tried though. I was a *little* bit stronger than him. The height thing would be tough. I would have to bring him down a few inches if I wanted to get my mouth over his-

"What?"

Fuck. I'd been staring off into space at Tailor during that whole introspection, and he'd noticed out of the corner of his eye. The Siamese Cat rotated in his chair to face me, and his expression was furrowed with expectation.

"Nothing," I said hastily. I hadn't done anything wrong. I was just thinking about some silly hypotheticals, but my roommate's green eyes were piercing. It was hard to not feel guilty about *something* when he whipped out his judgy face. With one scrupulous eyebrow raised that could have made me admit my every dirty secret if he pressed, Tailor observed, "You had that stupid look on your face."

"What stupid look?"

"The one when you're thinking about doing exceptionally stupid things."

I humphed and looked away. Tailor could be a real dick sometimes, and I was starting to feel less bad about my earlier off-color comments. I had to admit, though, it was a bit surreal. I'd just been thinking about how feasibly I could eat my own roommate. But until this year I'd never had to share a room with someone. I'm sure even a Predation prude like Tailor had thought about eating me sometimes, especially with how easily I got on his nerves. Oddly enough, the college had no rules against eating a roommate. After all, how could they possibly enforce that? That was probably why schools had a tendency to dorm up similar species together. Most predators weren't above devouring their own kind, but if they could bank on most people being about the same size it might cut down on occurrences. Though I'd heard the RA even say that roommate-on-roommate Predation helped keep housing waitlists low.

Tailor returned his attention to his work, and I returned mine to the pred forum. There was one final comment on the thread I'd been reading before Tailor's rude interruption. 'Most important: don't try showing off if you're inexperienced. Predding is impressive on its own. Take it from a seasoned veteran. Getting a whole dude or dudette down your gullet is tricky. No pred worth their salt will give you hard time if you can't do anything fancy.' Maybe I was projecting my current frustration onto it, but it honestly felt like that last response was said by someone like Tailor. If I was gonna commit to this, the whole point was to show off, make a big statement of my physical prowess and send a message to other predators on campus that the likes of Chance were not to be trifled with.

I folded my arms and grimaced at my laptop, imagining the commenter wagging a disapproving finger at me. Even though I wanted to acknowledge that these testimonials were coming from experts, if there was one thing I didn't like, it was being told not to show off. If I could gulp down some other freshman in front of the frat tonight, it would certainly put me on their radar. Joining a frat like Gamma Upsilon Tau would *definitely* bump up my street cred on campus. Eating someone at the party tonight was a short-term gain (pun not intended), while getting into that frat was the long-term goal. Why settle for being buff when I could really gain some weight to throw around (both physically and socially) by becoming a Gamma Upsilon Tau. Committing to becoming an active predator would really put me on some of the brothers' good sides.

One of my minimized internet tabs *bwoomp*-ed, and a little red icon popped into existence. Someone sent me a Furrynook message, which was unusual since I rarely used that. A 'request' icon prefaced the message accompanied with a picture of a familiar Boar. I accepted the message from him: Max Porkbelly (which couldn't possibly be his real name).

"Just picked up my pants from the laundry room. Thanks again, dude."

I typed a quick response. "Np."

After a short pause of loading dots, a return message appeared. "What's your room number? I'll slide a buck under your door once my stomach settles."

My finger hovered over the number pad, ready to type in the info, but then I had another idea. "How about a little favor instead?"

"You aren't gonna blackmail me, are you?"

I was about to assure him I had no such intention, but a second line popped up with a winky emoticon, and I knew he was just kidding. With the ice broken, I admitted, "I've never actually... you know... eaten someone before. I wanted to give it a try though and wondered if you could give me some tips? You seem to be an expert and all."

He replied with a smiley emoticon.

The pause that followed was devoid of the trio of dots that indicated typing, and despite his apparent flattered state, I wondered if he was actually going to say anything. I started to wonder if telling him I wasn't a predator was a good idea. What if he then decided I'd be better off as a prey the next time we were in the bathroom together? Eliminate the competition as it were. When the next *bwoomp* lit up my message box, a blue hyperlink to a popular porn site popped up. A message from him followed it. "Private Link. Be cool ok?"

Intrigued, I silenced my speakers and loaded the link. The title was just a date from earlier this year followed by a video file extension, but when the video loaded, I saw Max shirtless on a dorm room twin bed. I paused it instantly and then returned to the Furrynook tab. "What is it?"

"Consider it a beginner's guide," Max said. Then his profile pic icon grayed out. It wasn't like he was going anywhere, but he was clearly done with the conversation—probably still had a lot of Fox to churn.

I glanced over my shoulder. Tailor was still engrossed in his work, but I didn't want to risk him seeing. If this video was what I thought it was, and he turned around while I was watching it, it would be a whole thing. I grabbed my earbuds and moved myself and my laptop to my bed where I could rest against the cool brick wall. Once everything was all hooked up, and I was settled on my mattress, I started the video.

Max's room (I was assuming it was Max's room) wasn't that different from mine. It was just a bit messier in the laundry department, and books and papers flooded his desk haphazardly in the very far corner of the frame. The video must have been recorded at night as the only source of light seemed to come from the overhead fixture.

The Boar was shirtless with his familiar furry belly on display, but his thick thighs were stuffed into a pair of athletic shorts. He was still huge in every possible regard, but his belly looked flatter than it had been this morning before gobbling up the Fox. "Hey guys!" he boomed at the camera.

"Max, shhh!" someone hissed. The camera jostled back and forth and then resettled. A blurry face nosed in front of the lens. After stepping back, the other figure revealed himself to be a stout fluffy Bobcat who I didn't recognize—Gainsville U was a pretty big campus. "I don't want the neighbors to hear, okay?"

Max snorted on the bed. "Are all felines this obsessed with what people think of them?"

Wringing his paws, the Bobcat shuffled into the center of the room, right between the camera and the Boar. He wore cargo shorts and a green polo that clung to his slightly pudgy tummy. The footage quality was pretty mediocre; I imagined it was probably from a laptop webcam based on the shuffling sound it had made when the Bobcat bumped it. Still, I could see a fair amount of detail on the both of them. On the Bobcat, a flat gap of fabric stretched over the pit where his navel was, and he had a bit of a pointiness to his man boobs. His cheeks possessed a bit of extra roundness which I presumed wasn't just due to normal Bobcat ruffs. "I can't believe I let you talk me into filming this," he hissed with a wince. "What if my family sees this?"

The Boar rubbed his stomach and smoothed out the tight athletic shorts crimping his meaty thighs. "Yeah, that's my dream: showing my fat ass off to your mom and dad." Leaning onto his elbow, Max looked into the camera past the frazzled feline. "Ignore my roommate. Welcome to Max Porkbelly's guide to Predation. The little guy with fifty pounds of fluff is my roommate Je-"

"Max!" The Bobcat's fluffy ears stood up straight, and he

rushed towards Max with flailing paws, shushing the big-bellied Boar.

"Sorry. Meet my roommate, Nameless Paranoid Preyboy."

That didn't seem to ease the Bobcat any more. His ears flattened. "If this comes back to bite me..." He wagged his pudgy padded finger at his roommate, clearly wanting to add on some sort of threat, but as Max's grin broke wider, it was clear he had nothing and just let that weak trail-off linger.

Max shook his belly for emphasis. It was quite saggy and floppy, but I had a feeling that was about to change. "If I were you, I'd be more concerned what will come back to *swallow* you."

That comment elicited a blush from the unnamed roommate. "Yeah, that's exactly my point," he stammered. "It's hard out there for a willing prey. A lot of guys would take advantage of me."

"Oh come on, I've always wanted to film something like this. Think of it as an investment for future safe Predation practices in the future." Max waggled his brow.

With a huff, the Bobcat, whose name I guessed was probably something like Jerry or Jared, grumbled, "Alright let's just get this over with."

Pushing himself back upright, Max clapped his big hands together and scooted over on the bed. After patting the open space, the Bobcat sat down next to him, and the size difference became much more apparent. The top of the Jerry-Jared's head (not counting those big-ass ears) barely reached Max's shoulders. The Boar was also twice if not thrice as wide as the Bobcat (who wasn't exactly skinny himself).

"Okay, so as I was saying, this video is a little guide for all you hungry noobs out there who wanna whet their appetite on their fellow Furs. My preyslut of a roommate was kind enough to volunteer for a demonstration." He clapped his arm around the Bobcat and drew him close into a squishy sideways hug. Again, the feline's ears smashed down against his head.

With a huff, the Bobcat emphasized, "This is for those of

you who *also* wanna know what it's like to be on the receiving end of Predation. These techniques are recommended for those entering willing scenarios."

I grimaced, suddenly unsure if this would actually be helpful to me. I knew there were weird folks out there who fooled around with Predation as a past time. Usually it was friends who took turns eating each other, and then they'd let each other out before digestion could start. I had no interest in 'taking turns' with something like this. And over the past afternoon, the whole 'eat now and let out later' shtick didn't seem like it was going to get me anywhere. To me this was something you either committed to or didn't.

I was about to close the laptop when Max added, "You can also use some of this on less willing prey though." The Bobcat leered at his roommate, and Max upturned his palms innocently. "What? It's the truth."

The banter between the two went on, and I was starting to get impatient so I scrolled the timer icon to the right. The Bobcat got up and paced around the room in fast forward until it looked like something was actually going to happen. I resumed it when the Bobcat finally started shedding clothes, starting with his shirt, revealing a fluffy chest that was like a doughier version of mine. Then he dropped his pants, and I was getting a little uncomfortable, but thankfully he kept his underwear on.

"It's always nice to get clothes off if you can," the Boar commented to the camera. "Fabric can catch on your teeth."

"I also don't want these ruined in stomach acid," the Bobcat added as he folded his garments and laid them on the edge of the bed. "It'll take a while to start digesting a prey, but clothes will be ruined almost immediately."

"While some preds don't care either way, I much prefer the taste of prey when they aren't wearing all that cotton and stuff. It's a lot easier to gulp 'em down when you're enjoying the taste. I don't know *anyone* who likes the taste of clothes." The Boar snorted a laugh and smacked his belly. The Bobcat shivered and rubbed his arms, shoulders hunched and thighs clamped together. And while the Boar was already licking his chops in anticipation, I frankly couldn't relate. What made a Fur look tasty? How could you tell by looking? Maybe it was something you learned as you went. This video definitely wasn't the Boar's first time. That much was sure.

After a few tentative steps towards the big-bellied predator, the Bobcat retreated back. "I don't know about this, Max."

Instead of assuring his roommate, Max turned to the camera. "Prey can be really skittish, especially once shirts come off. This is normal, even if your partner is willing."

"Yeah," the Bobcat drawled. "I don't know how I feel about the implication of advising preds how to eat *non*-willing prey."

For a moment the friendly demeanor of the Boar cracked, and a flash of irritation crept into his expression. His ears twitched, and another snort grunted out of his frowning flabby muzzle. "Come on man, we talked about this be-"

"I know; I'm just having second thoughts is all."

"You've done this before," Max said which also piqued my interest. I shifted in my seat and sat up straighter.

The Bobcat splayed his ears and looked away from the predator. His eyes angled to the floor as uncertainty clouded his umber irises. I wondered what would happen next. There were still several minutes left of the video.

After a pause, Max heaved a sigh. He leaned towards one side, supporting himself with his palm squishing into the mattress, his thick arms like a trunk. "Okay. When eating a *willing* meal, cold feet is common, so the best thing you can do is to reassure them." Turning his attention back to his roommate, he added, "It's gonna be okay, buddy." Max sounded more annoyed than anything, but the Bobcat seemed to find something genuinely endearing in the Boar's apparent impatience to tuck his roommate into his gut. With the assuring pleasantries forced through tight lips, the Boar conveyed his brass. He was in control, and such assurances shouldn't even have been necessary, but he provided them anyway.

His big fuzzy ears perked up a tad. "Yeah?"

Max rubbed his belly, and the massive brown furry orb sloshed back and forth. "Yeah. You'll have plenty of room; I'm gentle; it'll be soft in there-"

"And you promise you'll let me out afterwards?"

The Boar smiled, but it wasn't a soft smile. Mischief breached the corner of his muzzle, just behind his tusk. I barely noticed it on the low quality of the webcam, but the Bobcat at his angle didn't seem to catch it at all. Maybe it was because it only lasted for a fraction of a second before collapsing into a more rueful grin. His chubby cheeks squinted his eyes. "Of course. You're my roommate."

My heart started pounding. I knew deception was often involved in Predation; not everyone could rely on brute force, especially in cases of minimal size difference. I knew what was going to happen. I had already seen Max with his belly bigger than it was in this video, and now I knew just who had made it grow since this was filmed—I checked the posting date—four weeks ago. *Oh shit.* I should have closed my laptop, or at the very least X'ed out of the tab, but Cat curiosity prevented me from looking away as the short portly Bobcat closed the distance to his exorbitantly gluttonous roommate.

Don't do it, I thought nervously, as if I was watching some bimbo open the basement door in a horror movie. The tension clenched my throat, and my heart pounded. Max sat up, leaned forwards, and wrapped his enviably beefy arms around his prey to draw him close. The Bobcat panicked for a moment, and he twitched nervously as his padded feet lifted off the ground. Max pressed his face close to his roommate's and slurped one of the Bobcat's fluffy cheek ruffs, and a strange mix of expressions flitted across the Bobcat's face: first revulsion and then... I didn't know what to call it. All of his features softened. His shoulders relaxed, and he slumped towards the predator. His eyelids got heavy, and the smile that split his muzzle looked... really into it. All the reservations vanished. It was like my dad when he had surgery, the way anesthetic turned him from a ball of stress into a zen master.

Max chuckled. "Yeah, you know you wanna curl up in me."

The Bobcat splayed his ears and blushed, like a full-on gay blush. I wasn't sure if there was something sexual going on; Max said he was straight, but he was certainly using some semblance of charm to get his roommate to lower his guard. With the Bobcat put at ease, the Boar licked his chops. Then it started.

Max stretched his jaws wide and made an exaggerated "Ooooowwwwmf!" sound as he clamped his mouth over his roommate's whole head. He shimmied his chubby hands down to the Bobcat's hips, taking a moment to readjust the feline's arms so that they were pinned to his sides.

I was so engrossed in the technique—the way Max planted his hooves on the floor and leaned forwards, the rhythm of bending his head low over his meal, shoveling gratuitous mouthfuls of Bobcat into his maw and then lifting back up on the swallow—that I hadn't noticed just how quickly and effortlessly he guzzled his snack. In only a matter of moments, Max had gulped his roommate up to his calves. I should have paused. After all, this was supposed to be research for tonight, but I couldn't stop watching the Bobcat's legs slip down into the Boar's slobbering maw. Max now had his head tilted all the way back, just like the forums had suggested, and his throat was bloated with the plump shape of his meal. I massaged my own throat, imagining the vicarious sensations of choking were my esophagus not just full but distended beyond belief.

Toes curling, the Bobcat's padded feet vanished between smacking lips. Max gulped, a deep *glurking* noise that sounded uncomfortable and plastic through the laptop's shitty microphone, but as the Boar slurped his tongue between and over his tusks, he seemed perfectly content. Meanwhile the neck bulge shrank as the mass of prey drifted down into the belly, causing the flabby orb to swell out enormously over his lap. "Ahh," he sighed. "Delicious." Max patted his belly for the camera as the large contents within shifted under the thick flab in large smooth lumps. He made tiny grunts as his prey got comfortable. I could identify the vague outline of the Bobcat-turned-dinner like an Anthro-sized bean. His head was on the upper right, and though his legs were undoubtedly tucked into his chest, his feet stuck out on the left. Max laid a hand on the head bulge and rubbed gently, and in response, the prey squirmed a bit.

"And there ya—*Uuuuoorrrrrrrrp*—have it." Though Max held an energetic gaze with the camera, I could tell his attention wanted to be on his gut. He massaged it with both hands now, shifting the form of the prey beneath his flab. He applied a light amount of pressure, fingers sinking into his doughy flesh, as he felt up the full shape of his meal. "And that's the proper way to eat a meal. I'll put a few more tips in the description. But if you did everything right, now you can relax and wait for nature to take its course, and before you know it, you'll have a belly enviable of all your fellow preds." He belched again, wet and loud. The spike of volume crackled the speakers, and there was no way his neighbors hadn't heard that when this had happened.

Then the belly started to squirm more fiercely. Max chuckled and patted the shifting head lump. I cranked the volume up to uncomfortable levels to try listening to the muffled sounds coming from within, but I couldn't make out any of the words. Max grinned. "Oh that's right. I *did* say I was gonna let you out, but... I'm having second thoughts." He rubbed his belly, speaking his words slowly and carefully. It was clear he'd already made his decision, but he spoke in a teasing way, acting like he was still on the fence. "I'll be honest. I've been wanting to pack your pounds on my gut since the first day. That chunky tum of yours has been driving me crazy."

After a long short bout of wriggles, the Boar replied, "Yeah I know we had an agreement, but if you're gonna let yourself get all plump and juicy like that, you should know that a hungry guy like me isn't going to be able to resist. And if you were out here, you would surely admit how good you look filling out my gut." Another pause. He nodded along to what his roommate was saying and stifled a short belch. He winked at the camera and held up one hand. He flapped his fingers and thumb up and down like a duck bill, the universal sign of 'This guy won't shut up.' Finally, Max interrupted the unheard monologue. "Look. You're just talking belly fat at this point, so accept it. I was hoping to keep you in there squirming for a while, but if you're gonna keep blabbering like this, I'll belch up all the air now." Hearing that must have sent the Bobcat into overdrive. He started to thrash harder. Smaller swells popped in and out against the belly's smooth surface like popcorn rebelling from a foil jiffy pop bag.

Max sighed and turned a slow gaze to the camera. "Well I think it's best to cut it off here. Join us next time as we talk about dealing with the annoyance of prey indigestio-*urrrrrrrrrrrrppp*!"

Holding his thrashing stomach in both hands, Max hefted himself off the bed and wobbled over to the camera. He flipped it off, and I was then prompted with a grid of more related videos from the site.

It took a lot to affect me, but God damn. I almost felt bad for the Bobcat, whose whole name I didn't now nor ever would know. Jerry? Jed? Jeremiah? It hardly mattered now. I thought about the big belly I'd brushed up against in the bathroom this morning right before Max gorged on that Red Fox. That was all that remained of the Bobcat. It was one thing to hunt, but to trick someone into willfully being eaten? That seemed kinda low. But then again... if someone willfully let someone swallow them, why wouldn't they expect to get digested? If anything, it was as much the Bobcat's fault as the Boar's for being stupid and gullible. I imagined even Tailor would voice a similar sentiment about making stupid decisions. At least unwilling meals put up a fight. If anything, that Bobcat deserved to get digested. I know I sure as hell would never crawl into a belly willingly.

Maybe it was because I was just watching film, and I had a tendency to not bother myself with what was already said and done, but honestly, I felt like taking Max's side. *Letting yourself get eaten? Pfft. That's just asking for trouble.* It's like setting a plate of warm cookies out in front of a bunch of toddlers with only a "Do not Touch" sign for protection. Toddlers are gonna steal cookies. Preds are gonna digest prey. There was no room for gullibility and stupidity in this literal eat-or-be-eaten world.

With digestion on my mind, my stomach gnawed like a gaping pit, and now I *really* regretted throwing away that wrap. That bag of chips and air had done nothing to ease my hunger. Deciding to take some of the advice from the forums, I grabbed my keys and wallet.

"I'm gonna go get lunch," I said flatly. I aimed my announcement more towards the general vibes of the room than the person I shared it with, intentionally leaving the presence of invitation vague. I walked to the door but held off a moment before opening it, waiting to see if Tailor would bite the hook. I didn't remember the last time he had gone this long without saying anything. Yeah, when he worked he would get in the zone and get tunnel vision for his monitor, but he would at least respond to what I said.

When Tailor finally picked up on the fact that I was waiting to see if he would like to join me, he spat, "Buying or hunting?"

"I'm just going to the cafeteria," I grumbled. When he didn't say anything else, I specified, "I'm buying it."

"Kay." He didn't sound at all appeased by my answer though. When he didn't say anything else or make any move like he was going to come along, I added to the tense passive aggressive atmosphere with a curt huff and left by myself.

I indulged in a burger and fries at the mess hall. It wasn't like I was trying to lose weight anymore. After I paid for my meal, I grabbed a seat by the window overlooking the campus quad. Dryness and dullness started to crisp over the lawns, and even in the open area, multi-colored leaves still littered the ground. It was less busy than it had been in the weeks prior. You used to see Furs of all sorts playing Ultimate Frisbee, reading, jogging, and sometimes even picnicking with paper plates and beach towels, but with fall fully cemented, activity was sparse. It was weird, like this was an entirely different campus than the one in all the brochures. I was promised liveliness, and now with each passing day, Furs became more and more reclusive as the Midwestern chills seized the land.

Eyes outside, I unwrapped my burger from its foil and lifted it to my muzzle. My nostrils flared of their own accord. God it smelled so good. I took a deep bite. It was shit. The patty was dry. The cheese was waxy. The bun was cold. I hadn't bothered with any condiments, but I doubted they could have salvaged the mediocrity of a college cafeteria burger. And yet, I still took another bite with just as much gusto. A shitty burger trumped a good salad any day. God, I missed eating junk food. I'd been abstaining all semester as part of Tailor's and my regimen.

My sensitive foot pads felt the vibration of clomping feet, and I glanced up to see a familiar face. "Hey, Cat."

"Max?" I was kind of startled to bump into him here, and my ears went back.

He laughed at my reaction. "Mind if I join ya?" He was already pulling out the chair across from me, so I didn't bother to say anything. The big Boar eased into the chair, and it creaked under his weight. His gut was still enormous from this morning, so he couldn't have fully digested his prey yet. "Don't worry, kitty," he whispered, eyeing my thrashing tail. "I'm not hungry enough for you. Besides, you and I are cool."

"I'm surprised you're hungry at all." I nodded at the tray he'd brought with him. Two slices of pizza, a bowl of cold greens, an oatmeal cookie, and a tall paper cup of fizzing soda occupied his tray.

Max rubbed the back of his head and smirked in that way of his that squinted his eyes. "I'm not actually, but..." He trailed off and patted his belly. "I thought I could do with an excuse to go out. I hadn't planned on eating in this morning, but damn that Fox was just so mouth-watering."

"You didn't have to get food to go out."

"Yeah but what else would a fatty like me do?" He laughed, and I nodded in assent. "So did that video help at all?" With one bite he chomped an entire slice of pizza up to the crust and sloppily chewed.

Again, I nodded. It didn't exactly give me any tips per se, but it helped to just watch an act of Predation from the safety of a dorm room. "So..." I didn't know how to ask this next bit. Should I be coy or brazen? I settled for miming both paws around my midriff, acting like I was jostling a belly as big as his and then pushed my paws in to hopefully convey the act of digestion. I mean... I already knew the answer to my question. It wasn't like I'd seen that Bobcat wandering the halls lately, but a macabre curiosity yearned to hear the predator admit it himself.

"My roommate? Yup."

My cheeks felt warm, and I glanced around to make sure no one would overhear us. It was late in the afternoon, so the cafeteria was pretty empty, and the nearest occupied table was engrossed in their own conversation. I don't know why it felt so conspiratorial. Especially since eating roommates wasn't against any rules. Maybe despite being allowed, it felt like it should be taboo. After all, bathroom Predation was banned because of the vulnerability of the space. What carried more vulnerability than living with someone? Eating a roommate felt like a bit of a dick move in my opinion, like it was too easy. How hard was it to gobble up someone who slept three feet away from you? I felt like a lot of people would agree with me. I wanted to establish some Pred-cred for myself, but I didn't wanna be an asshole to get it. Then again, Max didn't seem like an asshole, just really gluttonous. You kinda had to be, I supposed, what with him scarfing down a new meal on top of a whole goddamn Fox.

With his belly squished against the table, Max chuckled, making his drink slosh over the lip of the paper cup. "Care to share your deep thoughts, Socrates?"

Ears jerking up, I pulled out of my contemplative nosedive. "Just thinking about how arbitrary some of these dumb rules are."

"Yeah," Max agreed rubbing his belly. "Though I've never felt cleaner after how long I spent in those showers." Again, he chuckled. I worried that if his gut kept quaking the table, his Pupsi would topple. I wondered if he'd suddenly find me tastier looking if I was covered in sticky soda.

"So why *did* you eat your roommate?"

He shrugged innocently.

"Oh come on," I pushed. "Did he mess with your stuff? Did he play loud music? Did you just want your own room?"

Again, Max just shrugged. "There wasn't really a reason. I was hungry. He was there. He looked good. Plus, as we mentioned in the video, I knew he liked Predation. We even talked about it when we were moving in. I like to be open about it with people so they know what to expect. I told him I ate and digested people, and then he confessed that he'd been eaten a few times by old boyfriends. I think he had a bit of a crush on me to be honest. We already teased each other constantly that I oughta eat him some time, so I suggested we do a video for it."

"But then you digested him."

Max pressed his lips together, trying his best to look innocent, but a crack of a guilty smile betrayed him. "Yeah... you got me. I know lying like that was kinda shitty, but I was gonna eat him eventually. He was too tasty looking to pass up. I figured if I tricked him into it, he would at least have a good time going down." Max took a big gulp of his pop and then set it back down. The paper rim clapped on the plastic tray. "*Urrrp*. Ahh." The fizzy belch smelled faintly of vulpine.

"So who's your roommate now?" I didn't know a lot of people from our floor still.

Max rubbed the back of his head and looked away. "Uhhhhh... no one?" He forced a full-tooth grin, a grid of pearly whites between his yellowed tusks.

"You're supposed to report it if your roommate... well," I nodded my head towards his bloated stomach, "goes missing."

As if it was all some huge inconvenience, Max said, "Yeah but then I have to fill out the paperwork about it, and I'd have to check that box that said *I* was the pred, and they'd assign someone new to my room, and when the school knows you ate your own roommate, they try extra hard to pair you up with a pred the next time. I don't want that kind of competition."

"There *is* a video of you doing it though."

"Unlisted," he reminded me. It also seemed to be a thinly-veiled warning. Giving his tummy a gentle squeeze, he added, "*Right*, little guy?"

"I'm not..." I was going to say I'm not a little guy, but bristling didn't make something true. Max ate bigger guys than me for breakfast... literally. Instead I just slumped back in my chair and grumbled. "Right."

Max's expression softened. "Awe. I love how easy it is to ruffle you guys. You Cats really gotta learn to let things go, ya know?"

I nodded politely. Well, it wasn't politely. More like an eye-rolling uh-huh uh-huh kinda thing. His porky muzzle split into a lopsided smirk. A small guy like me was no stranger to a predator's teasing. Despite his jabs at my fragile ego, I felt like I could let my guard down around Max. He said we were cool, and I believed him. Leaning back so I could share his jocularity, I said "I thought it was in the nature of preds to 'not let things go.'" I waggled my eyebrows, hoping he'd catch my double entrendre.

Rubbing his belly with one hand, he pointed at me with his other. "You got me there." After a pause that let him slurp down more food, he belched and patted the table with both hands. "So. You're taking up the predator's mantle, eh?"

"I *want* to." I was a bit disappointed in myself that when I said it out loud to this experienced pred, that I didn't sound as convincing. Max seemed to notice that too, but he was nice enough not to razz me about it.

Instead he just asked, "Got a prey in mind for your first time?"

"Not yet. Should I?"

"It doesn't hurt. Especially if you're inexperienced. Honestly, it *might* be easier if you can trick someone into your belly like I did with my roomie, but that can be hard to swing. I'd definitely do someone you know though."

"Why?" I was steadily overwriting any remaining qualms I had with eating someone, but I wasn't sure if I wanted to do *that*. I could get over seeing a friend get eaten, but to do it myself?

"Isn't that... awkward? What if you guys have the same friends or something?" My circle of friends on campus was already really small, mostly just a few guys I knew a bit from the gym and a few classmates who I could tolerate because they weren't insufferable, pretentious professor pleasers.

Max stroked his chin. "I guess it depends on who your friends are. Mine usually don't care, and I wasn't friends with any of Jesiah's friends."

Ah so *that* was his name.

"It doesn't have to be someone you *like*," Max pointed out. He sipped more of his pop and then tossed the rest of that pizza slice in his maw. "I mean... it *can* be," he mumbled through the dough his teeth sloppily mashed. "I got no room to judge."

"You barely got any room at all," I said nodding my head at his belly. Max laughed, and the ease of tension felt good.

"All the same, I suggest you maybe eat an acquaintance at least," Max went on. "It's a lot easier to corner someone if you know their schedule. Plus, you wanna know what their social circle is like. I've sniffed out a good handful of willing prey on this campus, and most of them have a go-to predator who likes to keep things safe and calorie free. Swiping someone else's meal, even if it's not one they plan on gurgling, is really uncool. There's always plausible deniability, but it's better to be sure. And the last thing you wanna do is eat someone who may have a really big and hungry boyfriend or girlfriend. A little guy like you doesn't wanna make enemies on his first prey."

Making slow deliberate work of my fries, and stomaching the reiteration of my obvious smallness, I nodded agreeably.

After a pause, Max finally leaned forwards on his elbows. With a broad grin, he prodded, "So with that in mind, who's the first meal going to be?"

I pursed my lips and inflated my cheeks with a sighing puff. "I don't know. I really don't know a lot of people. I barely know the people in my own classes."

"It's past midterms."

I shrugged. I wasn't good at introducing myself to others.

I was better in social settings. You didn't have to learn a name unless you wanted to. "Maybe I'll try to get to know someone at the party tonight."

The Boar wrinkled his brow in confusion. "What party? The only party going on this weekend is the..." he trailed off into realization and widened his eyes. "The Gamma Upsilon Tau party?"

"That's the one."

"Look, Chance, I'm all self confidence, but... that is not a place to experiment. Parties at those frats have a sixty-eight percent survival rate. Literally. My stats prof showed us the math for a lecture once."

"That's not bad."

"Last party, the frat president Ross ate four guys just by himself."

"Stupid guys probably. Not guys like me." I jerked a thumb at myself. *Fuck, I was starting to sound like Tailor.*

"As your unofficial coach, I think you should set your sights lower."

"You don't think I can handle it?"

"I don't wanna be a dick, but let's be real here. You're like... really small. You're practically bite-sized yourself. Anyone there small enough to be prey for you will be rounded up for hors d'oeuvres before the first keg is emptied."

My ears started flicking. My tail lashed. The french fry I'd been holding snapped between my fingers. The jabs at my height were really starting to prickle. "I'm not *that* small," I argued. I was average. I wasn't tall, but I wasn't 'bite-sized.' With my ego boiling over, I crossed my arms and glared.

Hands shooting up in that universal non-confrontational manner, Max tried to backpedal his bluntness with more neutral-sounding advice. "The biggest mistake *any* new pred can make is biting off more than they can swallow. Trust me." I maintained my glower, and he rolled his eyes. "Come on. Look at me." He grabbed his belly and shook it. I could hear the sloshing inside it from across the table. "I'm fucking huge, and even *I* wouldn't push my luck at a Gamma Upsilon Tau party." Lowering his voice, "I'd literally rather risk suspension for not reporting my devoured roommate than risk them pairing me up with someone as big and hungry as me. Self-preservation is about smarts as much as size." *Dammit now even* he *was talking like Tailor.* In one remark he'd managed to emasculate me for my size *and* my intelligence, and it made my whiskers twitch.

In the back of my mind, a rational voice was trying to argue with the rest of my riled brain to listen to him, but he was the second person today to put me down, and this song was getting old. Who were these people to keep trying to tell me what I was and wasn't capable of? They've never been in my shoes. They didn't know what I could do. I could more than take care of myself. "This party is just the start of my plan. I'm gonna be part of that frat."

"You'll be lucky if you don't end up as part of a frat member."

"Gah, that's what my stupid roommate said." I got up and slammed my chair back into place against the table.

Max stayed in his seat. His ears were back, and he actually looked hurt. "I'm just trying to help. You had my back this morning, and I'm trying to return the favor."

"I don't know you," I sneered, "so stop pretending like you know me, or know what's best for me, or know whether or not I can take care of myself. Okay?" I picked up my half-basket of fries and dropped it on his tray of food. "I've had enough."

I left Max at the cafeteria and grumbled all the way back to the dorm building.

When night fell, it was time to get going. I spritzed some cologne under my arms, just enough to catch the girls' senses, and changed my shirt to a sleek black short-sleeve button-up. It form-fitted across my pecs and showed off the guns, and it looked pretty trendy. I didn't want to look like a nerd, but I didn't want to look like a T-shirt-wearing slob either.

When I left the room, Tailor was still working on homework (albeit a different assignment now). But when I got to the elevator, a chocolate-brown paw inserted itself between the doors right as they were closing. When they hissed back open again, Tailor was standing there with his arms crossed.

"Oh my God, you're not gonna talk me out of this," I growled.

Tailor stepped into the elevator next to me. "I figured. That's why I'm going with you instead." His eyes were narrowed and his voice was stiff.

I buried my face in my paw. "Ugh. No. Just... go do homework, you nerd."

"Fuck you. I'm gonna make sure you don't do something stupid... like get yourself eaten."

It was clear there would be no talking him out of it. He could be just as stubborn as I was. I pushed the button for the first floor and let the elevator rumble us both down to our destinies.

"Besides, I finished all my homework," he added spitefully.

Dick.

PART 2

We paused outside the Gamma Upsilon Tau house, just as we had this morning. While the curtains were all still drawn, now golden light shined through them as silhouettes with waving arms danced against them. Pounding music blared from inside. The front doors were open, and a few guys came running out. One, a Wolf, was shirtless with a bandanna around his head. Two other Anthros ran after him hooting and hollering: a Bear in a jersey and a tall Otter. Several guys and girls hung upside down from a tree in the front yard. A shirtless Orca with a big squirming belly sat at the trunk. His gut sagged over the waist of his khaki shorts. He was smacking his lips, and the people in the tree were pointing and laughing at the prey within.

"Yeah I can't imagine missing out on this."

I glared at Tailor's sardonic dismissal. Then I sighed. "You don't wanna be here-"

"Duh."

"Just go. I'll be fine, alright?" I stared him down, but he crossed his arms. My tail was lashing now, and I could feel my hackles lifting against the back of my collar, but I kept my voice even despite my rising anger. "I don't need anyone to take care of me, okay?"

"Is that what this is all about?" His brows knitted.

"Of course it is!" I shouted. A couple of the Anthros in the tree looked our way, but then resumed their own follies. I turned away from my roommate. I couldn't stand those eyes burrowing into me. "You're always on my case about everything. You may have grown up without parents, but I might as well have too. You still had guidance in your life, okay?" I shot him a nasty look over my shoulder. "I always took care of myself."

That was what pissed me off the most. It was like the last nineteen years of my life didn't happen. Here I was, standing alive and well in front of him, and Tailor seemed obsessed with this notion that I'd slip through the cracks of this big scary world unless I have *his* smarts and guidance, something only present in my life for barely two months, a constant nag foisted on me that I never once asked for. How could he look at me and not realize how well I've turned out, all things considered, and view me as little more than a feckless fucking kitten?

Tailor slumped his shoulders. He shook his head as a long, drawn-out breath spilled from his muzzle. "Chance," he began, and when he looked up at me, I felt the full brunt of his... I didn't know what to call it. It wasn't stubbornness. *I* was stubborn. It was like watching a Catholic find out that you masturbate. *Why can't you just do what I tell you to do so that I can feel certain you won't go to hell.*

I kept my eyes trained on him, my expression of neutrality and expectancy. *Go on,* I thought, *keep talking shit about me.*

But then Tailor's big green eyes welled up. His eyelids flickered as he blinked back tears. No. No no no. My resolve started crumbling. *You goddamn-*

"Do you have any idea how exhausting it is to constantly look over your shoulder? It is *so* easy for people like us to end up as meals for bigger Anthros. One time the heavy-set guy next to me in stats class's stomach growled, and... I don't even know if he's an active predator or just fat, but I ended up ducking out of class five minutes early just so I could get a head start out of the building, because I knew it would be open season otherwise, and I didn't want to take an unnecessary risk."

"Was he a Boar by chance?" I asked, thinking back to what Max mentioned about being in statistics. I mean, there are a *lot* of fat kids on this campus, but-

"Yeah, actually. How did you..."

"Yeah, that was Max," I said. "Probably was a good call to be honest."

"Fucking hell!" Tailor threw up his paws. A chubby Fox was coming up the sidewalk in ripped jeans and a too-small T-shirt. He was licking his chops with his eyes on the boisterous frat house. Thinking like Tailor, I led my roommate away from the walkway and out of the hungry predator's path.

Burying his face in his palms, Tailor mumbled, "This is fucking ridiculous."

"Jesus. Are you okay?" I asked.

"No!" He grabbed the collar of my shirt. "Why the fuck are you here? Seriously! If you get off on pulling reckless stunts, can't you just go skydiving or something?"

"Sorry, I'm afraid of heights," I spat sardonically.

"I'm just trying to look out for you."

"I didn't ask you to."

Tailor rolled his eyes. At least the threat of tears was over. "You don't need to ask people to care about you. That's not how it works."

"Yeah, maybe in Granny's house of privilege," I muttered.

Tailor just looked at me like *I* was being the unreasonable one. I didn't care what he did on his weekends or where he went to have fun or who he hung out with. Why couldn't he give me the same courtesy?

"Sorry, did you just talk to me about *privilege*, hetero?"

"You know what I mean. I was poor as hell growing up. I lived in a rough neighborhood. Ten percent of my *teachers* were ex-cons. Our geography books still had an East and West Germany. My hometown was so sketchy, that walking in pairs didn't help, because you wouldn't even wanna trust the people you knew."

"Hence, why maybe take my advice and be a little smarter

about all this."

"No, it means I can finally kick back and fucking relax. This place is a goddamn cakewalk in comparison."

"Doesn't change the fact that there are still a fuckton of fuck boys who will treat *you* like the cake. You realize that it's *because* of what happened to my parents that I worry so much, right? My grandparents are in their eighties. They made it that long because they were *smart*."

"So what? Your parents got eaten because they were dumb-dumbs like me? Is that what this is?"

"Fuck you." He looked away, his eyes peering into the night. His mouth was a flat line.

I broke the silence that followed his outburst. "You keep acting like being smart is the only thing that keeps people from getting digested and-"

"That's not what I'm saying. My parents were smart too, but-"

"Shit happens."

"Yes!" he exclaimed, as if he thought we were finally on the same page. We weren't though.

"Sometimes you're in the wrong place at the wrong time. Sometimes someone gets a jump on you." I thought about Stank wondering what exactly were the circumstances that landed him in a Tiger belly. He was far from valedictorian in high school, but I resented Tailor for insisting that his precious big-brain IQ made any difference.

"Yeah, and that's why we all need to minimize risk," he implored.

I rolled my eyes.

"Chance, frat parties are practically suicide for us smaller Furs. I'm just trying to be realistic here."

"You think you're better than me. That's what this is about."

"Yes. That's it. You know us gays. Just a superiority complex run amok." He sighed. "Look, Chance. I know what it's like to want a little more out of life. In my experience, it's not curiosity that killed the cat. It's ambition. We're descended from Lions and Tigers for Christ's sake. And you're not the only one who knows what it's like to always feel like you should be bigger and stronger than you are. So even though you're being a complete asshat, I'm not letting you go in there by yourself."

I stood there in the dark, feeling the chill of night ruffle the fur on my arms. Damn Tailor. He was so sentimental and... nice. And it was infectious, and I hated it. Where I came from, 'nice' wasn't a part of our lexicon. No one could afford that shit. We had to be cold and hard as the sea we fished from or the bigger metaphorical fish ate us. Everything was gray and grim there. And then along came Tailor with those big green eyes that have seen just as much shit as me but still managed to shimmer with compassion.

I raked the top of my head with my claws. "Okay. You wore me down."

"Better than having someone *break* you down."

I still felt emasculated at people insisting that I'd end up as prey, but I didn't want to argue anymore. We were here. I wanted to have fun. Pushing my pointer fingers together, I looked askance. "Listen, Tailor. About what I said before my shower..."

Tailor blinked, his face rigid and his muzzle flat. "I'm over it. I may be a skinny bitch, but, unlike some of us, I have thick skin."

I wanted to say more, but he returned towards the gap in the picket fence and started up the walk to the open double doors. I caught up with him and rubbed my arm. I still felt a bit guilty about it. I thought of what he'd said, and I could tell from Tailor's face that he was used to shit like that. And that made me feel even worse because I knew it wasn't fair that he should be. I wanted to do something to show my support, and without thinking, I grabbed his paw and linked my fingers through his.

"What the-" He shot me a confused glance.

"It doesn't bother me."

He yanked his paw away. "Okay. I get it. Now fuck off. If I'm gonna be stuck here all night, I don't want people thinking I'm taken."

We climbed the steps, and I grabbed him by the shoulder and led him to the side of the open doors. "That reminds me. Don't freak out, but if anyone asks, I'm gonna say I plan on eating you here at the party."

He backed away. "The fuck-"

I put up both paws. "I said, 'Don't freak out.'"

"I-"

"Shut up," I snapped. "Listen, I'm still planning on eating someone here. I don't know who yet; I'll see who looks good when we get inside, but I talked with a predator from our floor at lunch, and I found out that preds are more likely to leave someone alone if they think another pred has dibs. So if they know I'm a pred and they think you're my meal, it'll be safer for both of us."

Tailor rolled his eyes. "So like... an honor among thieves, huh? Fuck it. I've been uneasy since I got on the fuckin' elevator with you, so why the fuck not?" He threw up his paws and went inside. "Where can a Cat get a fuckin' margarita?" he shouted.

I couldn't help but chuckle as I followed him in.

Inside, the music was blaring. Within a few minutes my ears were ringing. Bodies were tightly packed in clusters all around the room. There were two couples (both of whom contained at least one man in a letterman jacket) aggressively making out on opposite ends of the couch, and considering one was a little Bunny with a big burly Badger, I had a hunch that kiss would be head-deep before the next song. And I was right. The next time we did our rounds of the room, the Badger was picking his teeth with the heel of the stiletto his make-out partner had been wearing, and the Bunny was replaced with a bulging belly.

"Fuckin' straight people, man," Tailor said to me in an aside. He had managed to get his paws on a sloppy slushy margarita in a red solo cup. He stirred the drink with a straw and took a tiny sip as we made our way to a less-packed corner of the room. I could smell the sourness on his breath.

The raucous behavior generated a lot of heat. That, mixed

with the ochre paint of the mostly bare walls, made it feel like we were partying inside a bonfire. A cocktail of the different species' sweat bombarded my nose. I could already tell that spritzing cologne on myself had been a waste. Tailor and I pressed our backs to the wall, not out of nervousness—well *I* wasn't doing it out of nervousness—but because I wanted to keep us out of other peoples' ways.

A female Wolf hopped onto the coffee table and started dancing. She kicked drinks onto the floor, but people still cheered. One male voice shouted, "Take your top off." She replied with a middle finger in that general direction and kept dancing. She was cute. Long brown hair a shade darker than her speckled chocolate fur swished back and forth. Most Anthros these days shaved down to their normal head fur. The feral look was in these days, but I still liked long hair on others. It was pretty and fun to twirl with your fingers.

"Seriously," Tailor went on. "Fuckin' animals."

"Okay, not all straight people-"

"I'm talking about in *general* now," he interrupted. He indicated the room with a broad paw gesture. Some Furs were grinding on each other. Others were passed out in chairs and covered in toilet paper. "This is like... once a month for these clowns. You really wanna live in this?" Tailor looked to his left where silly string and more TP tinseled a potted ficus. He reached in for something colorful and pulled out a bra between pinched fingers. "Ew!" He tossed it aside and then kicked it as far away from him as possible.

"People are just having a good time. Cutting loose. You should try it."

He brandished his margarita. "I'm already breaking the law, aren't I?"

"Oh no. Call the police," I sarcastically deadpanned.

"I'm surprised you're not already in your third beer."

"No alcohol for me tonight. It's good to stay sober when hunting," I said. *Besides, beer is for champions.* I'd celebrate with one once my gut was full. I wanted to have a clear head while scoping out my prey though, which I just realized I hadn't started yet. We hadn't been here long, but I'd spent every minute at Tailor's side. Max's advice about getting to know your prey nagged at me. But then again, at a party like this, it was probably okay, if not expected, for Predation to be a little sloppy. Hell, this was a perfect place to try Predation for the first time. Everyone was either distracted or drunk or both. Just because Max was successfully fat didn't make him an authority on the subject.

A Shark with a squirming stomach cha-cha-ed past us. He flashed his rows of teeth and winked at us. Tailor stiffened, but I nodded at the Shark appreciatively. "Nice catch."

His deep voice belched out, "I'm—*urrrrrp*—just getting started."

Just to be safe I put an arm around Tailor's shoulder and jerked my head towards him, in a 'me too' manner. Tailor looked away, pretending to be oblivious, and the Shark gave me a webbed thumbs up.

When the Shark was gone, Tailor crossed his arms. "I want no part in this."

"Would you rather a still-hungry Shark think you're up for grabs?"

"I'd rather be home catching up on *Family Guy*."

I lowered my arm and looked down at my feet. "Just go home," I said miserably.

"No."

"I don't need you dragging me down all night. You're being a wet noodle about this whole thing."

"The term is wet blanket, you dunce."

"You said it. Not me," I pointed out.

"I'll wear it as a badge for the rest of the year if you give up on this idiotic pursuit. You don't have to prove anything to me."

"Christ! This isn't about you," I yelled. I turned on him and pushed him against the wall. His eyes widened in shock. I jabbed my paws to my own chest. "This is about me, okay? *I* need to prove this to myself!"

With his spare paw, Tailor massaged his temples. He was

at his wit's end, but this was on him for thinking he could talk me out of it. He thought he was trying to be a good friend, but he insisted on trying to claim some nebulous moral high ground when he should really just get out of my way. I had nothing more to say to him as long as he was going to try lecturing me, and there was nothing more that he could possibly say that I would care to listen to. I left him in the corner of the room with a few prying eyes on him, and then I stomped deeper into the throng of partiers.

Stupid Tailor. The damn Cat got in my head. Normally a loud party like this was a perfect place to lose myself, but instead I was trapped within my own thoughts while a cacophonous whirlwind engulfed me. Everyone else around me was having a good time, and I just wanted to join them. This was my kind of element, and now I didn't feel like I belonged here. I knew that was Tailor rubbing off on me. I tried to distract myself by scoping out a potential prey. Maybe if I could scarf down someone, that would bring me some attention, and then I could acclimate into the vibe, more easily slide into a conversation.

I scanned the room. I spied a male Bunny across the room sipping a beer and laughing with a Coyote towering over him. He was slim but had strong muscular legs. The mental image of him hanging out of my maw with legs flailing gave me pause. I imagined one of his strong thumping feet whacking someone in the head, and then I'd look like an idiot. Plus, the Coyote he was with was bigger than me, and he might not appreciate some punk gobbling up his conversation partner.

There weren't a lot of people alone. The only loners were passed out drunks, and most of them were preds with full bellies, so they were off the table. Besides, eating someone unconscious was cheap. No one would be impressed by that. I knew that the forums suggested I shouldn't try to show off, but I still wanted to get an 'in' with this crowd. I thought about trying to weasel into a group conversation and wait for someone short to wander off.

Suddenly a paw gripped my shoulder and nudged me to the

side. A tall figure pushed past me. "Move it, dumbass."

I looked up to see the long-haired Wolf girl from earlier. She glanced over her shoulder and winked, and my first hostile instinct to challenge the person who'd bumped into me melted when I recognized her and realized she was just being playful. She paused and looked me up and down. I did the same. She had a rather broad muzzle for a female, but her large amber eyes kept her face angular and well-proportioned. She was slight of waist but broad of shoulders. Corded muscle twisted down her limbs. She was wearing denim shorts, the kind that were so short that the pockets stuck out the bottom. Her black top, decorated with a big rhinestone heart, exposed her fluffy white midriff. The low V at her collar showed off something more titillating.

"My eyes are up here, Tabby," she smirked. She put her paws on her hips.

"Yeah well..." I licked my lips. "Mine are only down here." I held my flat paw at my eye line which coincidentally was the same as her impressive endowments. Though not wanting to seem rude, I craned back my neck to look at her face. She was cute. I'd only ever been with other Cats in the past, but I wasn't too proud to imagine myself with a taller woman.

She touched my shoulder again and grinned. My eyes shot to the point of contact, and my heart started pounding. Guiding me, we sidestepped out of the middle of the room over by a table where some guys were playing beer pong. She leaned close. She smelled of sweat like most people here but also like strawberries. The sweetness and the saltiness combined hooked into my nostrils like harpoons. All thoughts of finding a prey fell out of the back of my head, and as she leaned closer my brain started flooding with desires for a different kind of hunting.

"I don't think I've seen you before," she yelled over the din.

I rubbed the back of my head. "Yeah it's my first time."

"Freshy?"

"Yeah. You?"

"Junior. I never miss a party here."

The fact that she didn't dismiss me right after finding out I was just a freshman was sending pumps of hopeful adrenaline into my veins. I combed the fur on the top of my head back with a paw, just to give myself a little tuft. "It's really wild. I love it."

The Wolf threw back her head and howled. It was a deep but singsongy *awooo* that could have earned her a spot as a backup singer for Lemming Lavato or Arianna Swande. Then she shook her head all the while keeping the smile on her muzzle. "This is nothing. At the End-of-May bash last year, the place was so packed, you could barely move."

I leaned back and grinned. "I bet the preds loved that."

"Oh you bet we did. I pigged out hard. On two Pigs no less. People called me Big Bad Ali."

Before I could stop myself, I appraised her fit figure again. "People call me Chance."

"Well Chance, I was gonna head upstairs. A couple of us were gonna have some fun and get away from the rabble-rousers. Wanna join us?"

My ears shot straight up. "Ohh! Heh. Y-yeah." I coughed away my stutter and salvaged a suave smile. "Sounds like a good time." She jerked her thumb towards the stairs, and I was about to follow when I remembered Tailor sulking somewhere. "I'll be right up. I gotta check on someone."

"Mmm. Avoiding a date to talk to little old me?"

I chuckled. "Oh no. Uh..." I leaned in and said, "I brought a snack with me for later, and I don't wanna leave him alone."

"Oh! Bring him up. I'm sure he'll have fun too. You know... until..." She chuckled away the trail-off, and I couldn't help but join her. It was an infectious laugh.

"I'll meet you up there."

Ali waggled her fingers and then sauntered through the crowd. Wasting no time, I darted through the room. So many of the guests towered over me, but I finally found Tailor by the disheveled bar. It was actually a mantle, but it did the job. His breath smelled of lime and liquor. His solo cup was full, which meant this was his second. I rolled my eyes. So much for looking out for me. I grabbed his paw and tugged him towards the staircase.

"Yo, what're you doing, man?"

"This hot chick invited me upstairs, and I'm bringing you along so no one eats you when you're all alone."

He wrinkled his muzzle and pulled away. "So you can ignore me on a different floor while you try to get lucky? No thanks."

"I don't wanna leave you alone, okay? Plus I gotta keep up the charade. I already told her I was planning on eating you, so if I don't show up with you now, then I'm gonna look stupid."

"How did men become the dominant gender on this planet? I swear you heteros would sell your kidneys for a chance at some piece."

My tail thrashed and brushed against someone's leg. They were bouncing up and down with a beer in paw, tromping to the music, so they didn't notice. My whiskers flicked. "You said you only came to keep an eye on me. If you really wanna let me go up all alone with preds, then you don't have any reason to stay here anymore anyway."

He set down his drink and rubbed his temples with both paws now. Through gnashed teeth, he grumbled, "You are such a *Cat,* and I hate you."

"Yeah, I figured. So are you coming up with me or not?" Ali was hot. If she was interested, I didn't wanna waste any more time letting someone else swoop in and get her. And I didn't mean pred-wise. Despite her pretty figure, I figured she could hold her own at this party based on what she already told me. And maybe if things went well, she could teach me a thing or two while I *played* with a thing or two.

With a shake of his head, Tailor sighed, "It's like I don't even know who you are anymore, man. Why can't you get obsessive about literally anything else?"

"It's not an obsession, man."

"You've talked about nothing but Predation all fucking day."

"I'm a college freshman. I wanna try new things. The fuck is wrong with that?"

"Because you want to eat people like me! I'm not just afraid you're gonna end up as someone else's prey. I'm afraid of what you're gonna turn into when you get a taste for other Anthros. This shit changes people. It's like a goddamn drug; it warps your world view. You stop seeing people as people and start seeing them as conquests and prospects. Everything stops mattering to those kinds of people except the thrill of the hunt, and the more prey they consume, the more it consumes them. With the exception of the last few hours, I've *liked* living with you, but I'm not gonna live with a predator. I spend enough time worrying about getting eaten on this campus. My room is the one place I feel completely at ease, and that goes away the second you turn into one of them. Choose now: this dumb endeavor or me. What's it gonna be?"

I couldn't believe he had the audacity to shoot this kind of ultimatum at me. The strong-arming only made me wanna eat someone more, just to prove him wrong about how much he thought he knew about Predation. "If you were really my friend, you'd just let me do what I want and get off my case."

"*Do* you think of me as a friend? Or just potential food?"

"I told you, I just said that shit to protect you, and if you haven't noticed, it's working. Not one person here has tried to sniff up either of us."

"We've also been lurking in the corners the whole time."

"So I eat one person at a party, and you just assume everyone's on the menu?"

"I've seen it before."

"Well you're different."

"Why?" Tailor demanded incredulously. "How? What makes eating me different from eating someone else?"

"Because you're my friend. Just because Max ate *his* roommate-"

"He did what?!"

"Just because *some* predators eat their roommates doesn't mean I would."

Tailor shook his head. "No no. Of course not. You'd just eat someone *else's* roommate. I get it. I'm the same way with petty larceny. I wouldn't *dare* steal from you, but some rando on the street. Yeah, daddy! Gimme that wallet. Don't worry, you can trust me around your stuff. I only rob *strangers*. That's you. That's how you sound right now."

"Jesus Christ! The Thanksgiving Day parade called. It wants you to stop raining."

"What?"

"I don't know. I'm fucking hungry, man. Just let me dance to the beat of my own drum, okay?"

Tailor's paws went up like he wanted to strangle me. He restrained himself, clenching his extended claws in the air in front of my face instead. His cheeks puffed out like he was about to start hissing. I didn't flinch though. "Are you just *trying* to be a spiteful, little jerk?"

"Don't call me little," I snapped. I pushed him back against the wall. Not hard, but he still lost his balance and thunked against it. His eyes got wide, and his jaw dropped.

"You know what? Fuck it. Fuck you. I'm done. Do whatever you want. That's all you care about."

He shoved past me, shouldering me in the process. He started to weave through the crowd towards the open double-doors. I groaned and followed him. "Hey! *Hey!*" I called louder. I caught up to him and grabbed his paw.

"Let go of me!"

I let him jerk his paw away, but he stayed. Maybe he was anticipating I'd come around to his idea. He crossed his arms, expecting an apology probably. He was sorely mistaken if he thought he was gonna get one, but I wasn't gonna let him make me the bad guy. I raised my finger in an aggressive point to tell him off, but as he raised his eyebrow, waiting for the shoe to drop, all of my anger deflated out of me in a drawn-out, exasperated sigh. "Fucking dammit, man." He got in my head again.

I turned away and folded my arms. I was pouting like a little kid, and that pissed me off even more.

He sighed in resignation too. "Look I get it. You wanna be

your own man. I'm not trying to control you, okay? I just wanna look out for you... *and* me. And I don't wanna be dragged along and watch someone act like a jackass. 'Cuz I can't put up with that."

"And I want you to trust that I'm in control. I've gotten everywhere by pushing my limits. I take risks, yeah, but I don't do it without thinking. I'm not stupid."

Tailor rolled his eyes. "You're a little bit stupid," he said flatly. Before I could argue, he added, "You've been pretty hard to like today. You deserve that."

"Fine."

"And okay. I'll trust you. But... if you're gonna do something, at least do it for yourself and not to prove something. You just look like an asshole when you do that. You wanna join a fraternity, join a fraternity, but do it for yourself, okay? Don't be one of those people who get double-dog-dared into rappelling down a mountain. That's how dumbasses go splat."

He was talking sense. And yeah, he had a point. "Okay. I wanna go try to at least get that girl's number. She's hot. She was flirting with me. I think I have a shot, and I don't wanna waste it."

Tailor eyed me skeptically.

"I'm serious. I'm progressive as fuck. I like strong spunky women."

The Siamese Cat looked from me to the stairs to the door and back to me again. When he finished his smart-brain calculations, he heaved a sigh. "Alright. I'll stay with you a bit longer. I'll go be your gay wingman or whatever, and then afterwards, we go home together. No eating anyone."

"Tailor-"

"I'm fucking serious, Chance. I'm not gonna be involved in that shit. I'm putting my foot down. It's not about whether I think you can or not or whatever asinine primal toxic masculinity bullshit compels you to be a jackass. It's about *me* deciding who my friends are and who will have *my* best interests at heart. Those are the terms."

I looked askance and grumbled, "Fine."

There were nine other Anthros there when we made it upstairs. At the top of the staircase, splitting off the two hallways of rooms, a huge open nook spread out. Across from us, a large window was blocked by curtains for privacy. The opposing walls each had a large deep couch pushed against the plaster with generic landscape art hanging overhead. One frame was crooked with a discarded pair of jeans dangling at the corner. A large open space between them once was occupied by a coffee table, but at the moment, the coffee table was upright and against the wall. Couch cushions and pillows were sprawled around for comfort as the group sat in a circle on the floor.

I spotted Ali in the corner, and she waved as soon as we reached the top of the stairs. "Oh hey! See, guys? I told you he'd show up."

They were a diverse group, about split evenly for guys and girls. Two Wolves counting Ali (the other a muscular guy with shaggy gray fur), a small portly Mouse girl, a trim Fennec guy, a butch-looking *thicc* Hyena girl (which I had to try hard not to feel was a stereotype), a big stocky White Tiger dude in tacky bling with a wide baseball hat tilted to the side, a chubby Pig girl in glasses (whom I tried to avoid eye contact with knowing what I knew about Ali), a girl Bunny with silver speckled fur and droopy ears (one of those larger varieties—some kind of European lop I guessed—so even though she was one of the smaller people in the circle, she matched size with the Fennec and I), and lastly there was the big-bellied Orca, still shirtless, I'd spotted outside when we first came.

The only one not in the circle, the Orca, was sprawled out on the couch, and despite it missing most of its cushions, he seemed comfortable lounging on his side with his head propped up on his arm. With the exception of the Orca, no one had a full belly. I noticed his wasn't moving as it had been earlier, which meant he'd either let his prey out, or they'd already passed out and started digesting in there. Ali scooted over and made room for me in the corner. I hopped over the open circle and took the place she offered between her and the other Wolf. Tailor rubbed his arm, standing right outside the circle looking uncomfortable.

"Sit wherever you want," the Fennec said from the other corner, and Tailor squeezed into a tight gap between the Tiger and the Pig right in front of the empty couch. The lop-eared Bunny and the Mouse sat across from them. The Hyena then closed up the circle on the other side by scooting closer.

"Ross, get in the circle," Ali insisted with a beckoning motion towards the Orca. We were already pretty tight together, so I didn't understand where Ali thought he would sit. He was the largest guy here, maybe at the whole party.

He waved his webbed hand. "Nah, I'm good. I'll be referee."

"Referee?" Tailor asked with a hint of nervousness.

The Gray Wolf brandished an empty green wine bottle. "Spin the Bottle."

Everyone in the circle pumped their fists in excitement.

"Why does Spin the Bottle need a referee?" Tailor asked.

"To make sure people don't try and chicken out," the Orca boomed. He smiled a broad toothy smile. His teeth glinted with ominous intrigue.

I leaned closer to Ali. "I didn't know people actually did this. I assumed it was just one of those sitcom things."

Tailor interjected with his paw in the air. "So... I'm hella gay."

"Who cares?" the Tiger laughed. "Nothing like that counts for shit in this game."

Ali nudged my shoulder. "You hella gay too?"

"Hella no," I said maybe too defensively. "But I'll play for tonight." Especially if I had a ten percent chance of planting my lips on Ali. And if luck wasn't on my side, maybe she'd be impressed that I'd be willing to kiss a dude and let me plant one on her afterwards. Alright, that was probably a stretch, but a guy can dream.

"I don't know..." Tailor started.

"You don't have to do anything you don't wanna do," the Pig

offered. She seemed sympathetic.

"Until the game starts," the Gray Wolf pointed out. "Then it's no-backsies."

"Come on, Tailor. It's just dumb fun." We both had an equal chance at kissing someone outside our usual wheelhouse. If I could suck it up, so could he. After so much stress and arguments, I think we both could have benefited from a stupid game that we could laugh about later.

"Goddammit fine. Deal me in or whatever."

"I'm going first," the Gray Wolf decided.

"You always go first," Ali complained with a rueful smirk.

"I drained the bottle. I earned this."

He leaned into the circle, and it was then I realized he actually did seem a little tipsy. Bracing himself on one paw, he plopped the bottle in the middle of the circle. He paused and looked up at Ross. "Pass me that pizza box." Ross sat up with some difficulty and saw where the Wolf was looking. The empty box was draped over the far arm of the couch with no regard for the upholstery. Ross couldn't reach it, but the Mouse could. She snatched it and slid it greasy side up to the Wolf who flipped it closed so the residual cheese and sauce couldn't smear into the carpet and then hammered it as flat as he could with a fist.

The canine set the bottle on its side and with two fingers against the neck, he gave it a hearty spin. It spun a lot better on the flattened cardboard than what would have been possible on the shag carpet, but even then, it didn't reach as many spins as I'd seen on TV shows. So when it landed on the Fennec after two rotations, it felt a bit anticlimactic.

"Fuck!" the Fennec shouted.

I nodded to Tailor. "See? You got a good chance at some gay action."

The Fox however had stood up. "No way. No no no!"

"Sit down," Ross demanded.

"This isn't fair!" the Fennec yelled.

Now everyone was making noise. The Furs in the circle were rolling their eyes and throwing out aggravated bits of two cents.

"Man up." "What did we *just* talk about?"

It made me a bit uncomfortable and undermined what I'd just reasoned with myself about how something low stakes was what Tailor and I needed right now. I didn't know any of these Furs though, so I didn't want to throw my own voice into the dissonance, but this was the first turn and it was already a shit-show.

That didn't stop Tailor from saying something. He leaned into the circle trying to talk over the others. "Come on guys, if he doesn't wanna, he doesn't wanna. Don't force him."

"If you're willing to play, you play by the rules," the White Tiger snapped at Tailor, and my friend scooted away from the angry pointing claw.

"What happened to 'It's just dumb fun?'" he grumbled.

Ali crossed her arms. She looked at Tailor but the edge in her voice was obviously targeted at the Fennec. "There's no game to have fun *with* if people act like little bitches when it doesn't go their way."

"Come on!" The Fennec whined. He flopped back down, and as all eyes trained on him, he scooted out of the circle and into the corner of the nook. His eyes conveyed a desperation so intense that even *I* thought he was going overboard. This was the kind of fragile hetero bullshit that Tailor normally rolled his eyes at, so it was weird that my roommate was the one trying to convince the others to let it go. If I had a high chance of kissing a dude, then this guy should deal with it too. It's not like they had to tongue each other. But as the Fennec's lower lip stuck out in a pathetic whimper, and the others started crossing their arms and razzing him further, even I had to admit this seemed like it was getting out of paw really fast.

"This is the first time I've ever even played!" The Fennec whined. "I can't-"

Ross sat up, and the simple act of shifting his weight was enough to silence the whole group. The massive Orca jerked a thumb at himself. With leering eyes he seized control of the chaos and, with a rumbling commanding voice like a splitting boulder, authoritatively enunciated, "Referee."

"Ross, come on," the Fennec pleaded. He rose up to his knees and hobbled towards the edge of the couch. "I thought we were bros."

Ross was unfazed by the appeal. "You chose to play. You wouldn't be complaining if it had landed on anyone else. So nut up and get it over it. Or I'll settle it personally."

The lingering threat seemed to break up all remaining retorts that were on the Fennec's tongue. The small skinny vulpine slumped his shoulders forwards. His head hung low as he sat back on his ankles. The Gray Wolf who had been mostly quiet during this tumultuous discord cracked his muzzle into a wicked grin. He curled his fingers and licked his lips, eyebrows waggling. "Come here, pretty-boy."

The Mouse leaned in and clapped him on the shoulder. "Go on. Have some pride, huh?"

With a wince and a gulp, slowly the Fennec crawled into the center of the circle on his paws and knees. He smacked the bottle as he passed it, and it spun towards Tailor. I bet *Tailor* would have been happy to have been the one chosen for round one. The Gray Wolf had a good jock body that even I could admit I was pretty envious of, exactly Tailor's type.

Ali leaned towards me. Out of the side of her mouth she muttered, "Pussy."

I smirked. "I'm glad I'm not that insecure." I took a risk and walked my fingers up her thigh. "Though I can think of someone else I'd love to have the bottle land on for my turn."

Ali laughed and patted my head. "In your dreams."

I froze. All the playful banter we had exchanged before I came up here soured in my memory. I lowered my paw away from her before things got even more awkward. I really thought-

"Come on, Abe! Please! Please don't make me do this," the Fennec whispered. He was kneeling right in front of the Wolf now. The Gray Wolf, Abe, had spread his legs and leaned back, supporting himself on one paw. His eagerness overpowered the vulpine's hesitancy.

Abe curled his finger again and ignored everything the smaller Fur said. "Come to Papa."

The Fennec flinched.

"Jesus. It's just a kiss," I muttered.

Ali chuckled. "Yeah I guess that's a good way to think about it."

I tilted my head at her to ask her what she meant, but then the circle started chanting. "Do it. Do it. Do it."

Fists bobbed up and down as the Fennec leaned closer and closer to the nonchalant Wolf.

"Do it. Do it. Do it."

Abe tucked his knuckle under the Fennec's chin drawing him close. They were almost muzzle to muzzle. The Wolf's grin split open, revealing gleaming fangs. The Fennec on the other paw had tensed from nose to tail. His teeth were gnashed in a wince.

"Do it. Do it. Do it."

The Wolf opened his mouth wide. The paw that had once beckoned the Fennec to his fate now guided it. Wrapping fingers around the base of the vulpine's skull, he yanked forwards, and with what had to have been practiced ease, popped the Fennec's whole head into his muzzle. I froze. The chanting didn't stop; it just crescendoed with more energy as Abe clamped his jaws around the Fennec's neck and pushed himself forwards. His cheeks puffed out as he stuffed in the Fennec's shoulders. The Fennec started squirming, but in a hunching pounce, the Wolf pinned the smaller Anthro's arms to his sides.

And I realized with horror that what I had thought was a harmless make-out game had proven to be a game of Predation. "Oh shit," I murmured, though no one heard me. Everyone else— well, everyone besides Tailor—was making exuberant noise of support as if cheering on the school football team. I couldn't take my eyes off the hedonistic display of submission and power. It turned so much of what I'd learned today on its head. I always thought of Predation as chaotic and messy unless it involved some sort of deception like what Max did with his roommate. This was a group of friends—I assumed at least some of them were friends based on the sense of familiarity—performing the acts like regulated procedure. Hell, they even had a referee, and now I knew why. Suddenly the Fennec's protests seemed a lot less hyperbolic.

I was too stunned to say anything. My brain was on pause save for one thing: observing the expertise of the predator's technique. The way the C's of his thumbs and index fingers notched perfectly on the Fennec's wrists to keep everything straight. The way he undulated his tongue slightly past his jaws to draw in his prey. The way he hunched his shoulders to create a smooth arced path from mouth to gut.

While everyone was cheering on the ingestion of the Fennec, I was mesmerized. I started to suspect that Tailor was right after all. Had I *really* wanted to be a pred before, or did I just want to show off and seem like a tough guy? Witnessing the adulation this Wolf received as he gulped down his prey changed that. It was one thing to watch one of Max's videos and read encouraging comments from faceless web avatars. The sheer power this Wolf displayed... I wanted that. I think that this is what it means to *want* to eat someone. All day I'd been, as Tailor said, obsessed without really appreciating it for the act it was. I was an outsider looking in. I viewed it like an easy alternative to working out, because Tailor had challenged my ability to take care of myself in this voracious world. It wasn't because I wanted to be a predator, but because I was fed up with people treating me like prey.

With the Fennec Fox's neck slurped into oblivion, everything clicked. People like Tailor viewed Predation as something roughneck and classless, like it was an impulse of animalistic drives that drew our kind down to the uncivilized level of our feral counterparts. It was like when people looked down their snouts at people from my old high school. The way Tailor looked down his snout at myself and the loud raucous partiers that surrounded us. But Tailor just couldn't appreciate what made people like me tick. Gay or not, he bore a special kind of class privilege. Anyone who didn't spend all their time in cozy spaces with a muzzle buried in a book was riffraff to people like Tailor. I looked around this party and I didn't see vacuous animals. I saw people finally relaxing, finally cutting loose, finally indulging in a need to scream when the world says to sit still and be quiet.

Predation wasn't the activity of the uncivilized. It was the liberation of free spirits, ready to howl at the moon and say, "This is who I am, and no one can shame me for it." Tailor of all people should have seen an appeal in that. I wanted that liberation. I wanted to march around the world and not give a flying fuck what anyone thought about me. I was gripped by a new fantasy to sit in the center of a circle like this and be admired for that specialized strength, not of muscle or size, but of spirit and character.

I was sure if Tailor heard these thoughts of mine, he would say something obnoxious like, "But then you're still doing it for *them*." He'd say it just like that, with a spiteful emphasis on 'them,' as if 'them' was something only a crass fool would want to be like. Tailor didn't understand what I wanted and needed. The attention and praise from others *would* be for me. I wanted a sense of community that would encourage me rather than clip my wings. It should have been obvious that Predation is about the predator, not the prey. I never felt comfortable in my own skin because I was trying fruitlessly to sculpt my body the way a prey would, the way prey told me I needed to be.

Even Max said this morning that he couldn't resist the taste of a lean muscly guy, despite his own straightness. Whether you were as chunky as Max or Ross or as lean as Ali or the other Wolf, Abe, didn't matter. It wasn't about what you could strive for with your body, but what you could do with it as is. I could stroll into a room, and everyone would see me for what I was, not what I 'could be' if I 'only applied myself.' Fuck that. This group knew what they were doing. They knew who they were. Their roles were so concrete they could literally gamble them. I caught the Gray Wolf's face. His eyes were zeroed on his meal's back, and the sheer indulgent joy shining through the crack of the stretched jaws was all I needed to see to know that I wanted this too.

I glanced down at the wine bottle on the hammered cardboard, and I could feel it calling me, begging me to give it a spin and let it choose a meal for me. Max warned me to be careful at this party, but here and now, surrounded by people egging on this very behavior, was the perfect opportunity to finally try Predation for myself. The playing field was as level as the pizza box smashed into the carpet.

With another loud gulp of flesh, I pulled myself out of the tantalizing spiral into delusions of grandeur and returned my attention to the extravagant show of predatory force being exercised only a few feet in front of me, a more intimate distance than I had been when Max ate that Fox this morning. I couldn't have been closer to the action unless I was participating.

For every inch that Abe drew his prey into himself, he thrusted himself over his prey. Rising to a crouch, the Gray Wolf exerted all of his strength—his biceps and thighs quivered as though benching weights—downwards over his meal. His jaws stretched wide as he descended over the thin Fennec's upper body. He gulped every few inches, and his throat made hard *glurking* sounds. An enormous bulge swelled out the front of the Wolf's gullet, and his eyes rolled up into his head. "Ohmmmm," he groaned. His tail wagged, and even my own mouth watered. The pleasure on the Wolf's face tempted me with curiosity to know the taste of vulpine. *Damn, I love Foxes,* Max had said this morning before gorging himself.

Once the Wolf had swallowed up to the Fennec's stomach, with arms thoroughly pinned to his sides by the tautness of jaws, Abe collapsed back on his butt and tilted back his head. The Fennec's legs dangling out of his mouth twitched and spasmed. His toes curled. His feet twisted on flailing ankles as he wriggled down the front of the canine as a stretched-out lump. Abe cupped his paws to his throat, and with one final gulp, the Fennec's feet disappeared behind a clack of teeth, and the panicking form descended into his midriff. A huge orb ballooned out as the weight bounced into his lap. Thumping a fist against the center of his chest, Abe uttered a low, long, cross-eyed belch, and everyone cheered.

Everyone except Tailor.

Encumbered by the extra weight in his stomach, Abe clumsily clambered to his feet and took a teetering bow.

Tailor shrieked, "Why would you do that to him!"

Ali shot Tailor a patronizing sideways glance. "Uh... because the bottle *pointed* at him."

"That's not how Spin the Bottle works! You're supposed to just... kiss or whatever."

Now aware of the meaning of Ali's joke, 'thinking about it as a kiss,' I leaned back against the wall, removing myself from the confrontation. Ali and Tailor both leaned in though.

"That's Spin the Bottle for pussies. Did you seriously think that's what we were doing? What are we, eight?"

"Well *one* of us was ate," the Pig quipped with a snorting chortle.

Tailor wrinkled his muzzle. I could tell he found that joke, for lack of a better word, distasteful. With pleading eyes, he turned his attention to the other Wolf. "You're gonna let him out afterwards, right?"

Abe rubbed his big belly with one paw and picked his teeth with the index claw of the other. His eyes were glazed over, complacent and content. Between the booze and the predatory high, he hadn't even noticed he'd been addressed. The Mouse kicked him in the ankle.

"Hm?" He jerked his attention back to the group, and Tailor repeated his question with a bit more emphatic desperation. The Wolf belched. "Why would I do that?" It wasn't a taunt or a tease. The Wolf seemed genuinely baffled by such a request as he continued rubbing his stuffed gut. His paws roved over the rises and falls of paws pushing out from inside.

Tailor threw his arms out towards the shifting form of the Wolf's stuffed belly. "That isn't Spin the Bottle!" he squeaked. "That's... that's fucking Russian Roulette!" He stood up on shaky legs. He was obviously distressed. "Let him out!"

The Wolf burped again and quirked an eyebrow in disbelief. "Yeah... no."

"This is barbarism!"

Ali rolled her eyes. "This is the world. We're just making it more fun."

I tried to keep my own expression stoic; I wasn't keen on adding my own voice to the ruckus, but the look of abject horror on Tailor's face radiated waves of guilt into me. This was exactly what he'd said he didn't want to bear witness to when he promised to stay. I didn't know what to say though. To be honest, I didn't know what I *wanted* to say. I'd just witnessed Predation, and my veins were still pumping endorphins through me. I couldn't have echoed Tailor's emotional state if I tried. While his heart was currently pumping him with a heavy dose of fight or flight fright, I couldn't douse the fiery thrill keeping my ears up and keen. Then, for a moment, we locked eyes: Cats, roommates, friends, and I knew he expected me to speak up, and my silence conjured a look of sheer betrayal on his muzzle. Tailor shook his head and turned to leave, but the White Tiger grabbed him by the tail.

"Whoa there, lil' kitty Cat. Where you think you're going?"

Tailor yelped and stumbled backwards. He spun back around and yanked his tail free and clutched it close to his chest. "I'm not going to be involved in this!"

There was a second uproar from the rest of the group, bigger than the protest against the Fennec. "That's not fair." "That's not how this works." "You can't leave now!"

Tailor tried to turn away from them, but the stocky Hyena girl stood up and stepped in front of him. Paws on her hips she leaned left and right to block his path as he tried to get around her. Her toothy grin grew wider.

"Move! Let me by!" Tailor demanded.

That was when Ross sat up again. The sound of the couch springs coiling and uncoiling beneath his girth once more silenced the whole group. "Sit down, Cat." Tailor whipped around towards the Orca, a retort at the ready, but the big guy cut him off with a glare. "Here's how this goes down. Once the game starts, everyone commits. With every passing round, the game gets more intense. That's the whole point of it. He-" Ross pointed at the wriggling sphere of a belly- "was the unluckiest of us all. He got eaten first when the circle was fullest. So, if he has to commit when the odds were in his favor, then everyone has to commit, and leaving when the game gets harder not only ruins the game for others, it *condemns* others. It's not fair to those who remain to have their chances lowered by lack of participation. That's why no one leaves."

"This isn't a game!"

"It is though. It's all a game." The Orca raised his upward palm to the sky and looked up into the distance as if preparing a soliloquy. "Life is just a game."

"Not the way I play." Tailor put his foot down. "Chance," he called.

I gulped as all eyes trained on me. *Dammit, don't bring me into this.*

Ali propped her chin on her paw. Her soft eyes fanciful and expectant.

"Uhh..."

"Chance, you aren't seriously okay with this, are you?" His words were pointed, sprinkled with anger and fear. There was a hidden subtext: a 'What did we just fucking talk about?' tone that I was clearly supposed to pick up.

It would have been so easy to say, 'No,' and lie for his feelings, but as more eyes turned toward me, the sensible lie was caught in my throat.

"Oh. My. God," Tailor berated.

"Alright, alright," I rushed out to save face. "This isn't Tailor's scene, and I promised I'd take him home." I was met with boos when I stood, and they stung like fishing hooks barbing my skin, trying to reel me in with disappointment. But as I shot a glance at Tailor, it felt different. It was like *he* was the real fishing hook, dragging me out of my pond. My morbid curiosity and the resurgence of my predatory desires urged me to stay.

"You're not leaving," Ross rumbled.

"Like hell we aren't." Tailor's muzzle was pursed, and his whiskers twitched.

The White Tiger stood up now and stepped between Tailor and I. The Hyena hadn't backed down either. Ross grinned. "There's no chickening out here. Once you commit, you commit."

"I'm not some cult member. I don't have to do anything," Tailor growled. His short white hair started lifting up on his hackles out of his shirt collar.

"And we don't have to let you leave," the Hyena sneered.

I started to worry things had gotten out of control so I put up both my paws. "Okay, okay, guys. Let's be cool. Tailor didn't know what this was." Granted I didn't either, but I didn't want them to think that. "He's not into this sort of thing."

"Well yeah, no one *wants* to be prey," the Mouse girl chimed in from her spot on the floor. "That's the point."

"Then why would you play-" but Tailor was cut off.

"That's the game," Ross rumbled. "It's *always* a game whether you do it here in a circle with a bottle or out there-" the big Orca pointed towards the drawn window curtain- "with your own wits. You could just as easily get eaten on your way home from this party by a pred lurking in the bushes. In fact, that's a typical strategy for freshies. They win. You lose. And there's no opting out of that either."

"Fuck you," Tailor growled. "Come on, Chance, we're out of here. And if you keep us here-"

"You'll what?" the Orca challenged. His broad mouth split into a toothy smirk. "Amber's right." He nodded at the Hyena. "We don't have to let you leave. This is a frat party full of hungry preds. And your odds are actually a lot better if you stick around. This is a game of elimination. You either eat or you're eaten. Once one of those happens, you're done. Fifty-fifty for all of them. But if you skip out now. I'll eat the both of you, and that's a guarantee."

"You can't do that!"

Ross lowered his head and waggled his eyebrows (or his hairless leathery versions of eyebrows). "I'm the referee."

I had no doubt that Tailor could outrun this massive blubbery Orca, but with all of these other fellow preds around, he'd be hunted down with ease. "Sit down, Tailor," I said.

"Chance-"

"Sit down!" I led by example, plopping back between the two wolves: one full and one hungry. He looked down at me, so betrayed. I led him into this, but if he wanted a chance at getting out of this, he was going to have to play along. I didn't doubt that Ross would follow through on his threat. Wringing his paws, Tailor sat down, legs tucked into his chest and tail curled around his shins.

Ali looked off into space with a determined leer. "So that's what you meant about your little comment," she stated. All of these seasoned predators would have had senses keen enough to hear her low voice, but it was directed solely at me, and it still felt private as everyone retook their seats and argued over who was going to spin next.

"Huh?"

"You thought we were just kissing."

"I-"

She chuckled. "I thought you were just arrogantly assuming you'd be able to down all of this." She roved her paws down her sides and flashed me a mischievous grin. "Don't get me wrong, I'll honor the game, but some people just don't have the spunk and moxie to actually do it... especially someone... larger than them." Her words were knifed with omen as she sized me up. In an idle motion, she scratched her stomach below the hem of her belly shirt, and I saw what could be my future.

"I wasn't-" I tried to argue. I didn't even know where I was going with that sentence, but Ali cut me off.

"You're full of shit." Her flirtatious grin faded into a straight line. "I actually thought you were a serious predator. You said you were going to eat him." She pointed at Tailor. "But that was clearly a lie. You're fake as fuck. Unless you want to surprise me."

Ross settled the debate of who goes next with a randomizer app on his phone. He showed us the screen which featured a wheel with equal-sized pie slices: Tiger, Wolf, Pig, Mouse, Bunny, Hyena, Cat, Fatter Cat. He tapped the start button, and it whirled in a swirl of colors. When it stopped, the little screen erupted with an animated confetti pop as the needle pointed straight down at the Bunny slice.

The Bunny's ears shot straight up in the air in excitement before flopping back down as she folded her paws in prayer. "Yes! Thank you! Thank you!"

Amber the Hyena grunted. "Don't thank the wheel yet. You could get Drake and end up right back where you started on the menu with the rest of us."

The sizable White Tiger snickered and cracked his knuckles.

"What?" Tailor asked with a slight squeak. "What do you mean by that."

The Bunny fluffed up her cheeks. "Amber's just being a bitch. I can take any of you."

The chortle that moved through the circle tarnished the vote of confidence. In response to Tailor's spoken—and my hidden—confusion, the Pig explained, "If you can't swallow your prey, they're still in the game. Which means so are you, and play continues."

Drake the Tiger flexed his muscles. "And I'm a *thicc boi*."

"Unless Angela's really stretchy, she probably won't be able to eat half of us," the Pig stated.

"Shut up, Bianca," the Bunny—I assumed she must have been Angela—snapped at her.

Tailor exploded. "What!? Why would you guys bother then?" He looked at the Bunny and the Mouse back and forth repeatedly. They were the shortest ones here.

The Mouse shrugged. "You know how hard it is to overpower someone when you're a Mouse? A game like this is my best bet to get some prey. If I tried to eat someone out there-" she pointed towards the wall, indicating the big, scary world beyond-

"more than likely it'd get turned around, and I'd end up in the stomach."

"But you could-"

"Lose? Yeah." The Mouse didn't seem fazed by that concept. "It's like Ross said. The whole world is win-lose. If I can get some pred cred in here, even in a game of chance, it'll make me less likely to be a meal for someone else later on. Stakes are high, but they always are." Looking across the circle, I could tell by Tailor's wide green eyes that he thought the smaller Anthros here were even crazier than the big predators. Personally, I couldn't see how things could end well. There was a fifty percent chance they would get eaten from the fickleness of the bottle before they even had a chance to try being a predator themselves. And if they failed to down one of the others on their turn, the fact that they could just as easily end up as prey the very next turn gave me vicarious anxiety. If I were them, there would have been no chance in hell I could justify a risk *that* big.

The Mouse—I still hadn't caught her name—talked as though being prey was inevitable. I mean... it technically was. There'd been studies about how soon or late in life people were likely to get eaten. Just earlier today I had been thinking about the fates of my own friends from high school. I supposed some people like Tailor wrestled with the notion of becoming prey more than others. Those worries had been spurring a lot of my decisions lately. That was what got me to the gym, and it was what landed Tailor and I in this predicament. A game like this didn't seem like an effective option, at least for them. It was like someone trying to escape poverty by putting all their faith in the lottery. Except losing this cost a hell of a lot more than two bucks.

As Tailor had put it, this was still a game of chance, Russian Roulette. Maybe Tailor had gotten into my head again, or maybe thinking about how low the chances were for these couple of smaller Anthros to make it through the game stifled my previous convictions. With this new concept of size and the chance of failing to 'win' the game weighing on me, I knew that the Mouse wouldn't be able to eat me, but what if all the smaller prey got eaten before I even had a chance to spin? I locked eyes with the other predators like Drake the Tiger, Ali the Wolf, and Amber the Hyena. Ali seemed confident I wouldn't be able to swallow someone her size whole, and I believed it. This made the game a lot more complicated. There was a very real possibility that this could be my last day on Earth, and there was nothing I could do about it. For a brief moment, I naively thought that this was order, but it was just organized chaos enforced like law.

That was when Angela crawled into the center of the circle. Her big teeth gnawed down on her bottom lip as she spun the bottle. It went round and round a few times. While the big preds leaned back with lax and apathetic expressions, the others crossed their fingers. Tailor looked livid, and guilt started building up in me. What if the bottle stopped on him? He was a twink. The chunky Bunny might be able to choke him down, even if he put up a fight. I didn't want to think about what I would do should that come to pass. I just silently hoped it wouldn't happen.

When the bottle stopped on Ali, I heaved a sigh of relief for Tailor and me. The big brown Wolf grinned, and the Bunny cursed. Leaning back with her arms crossed behind her head, Ali extended her legs into the circle with confident casualness. She crossed her ankles and sneered, "Alright, Cottontail. Give it your best shot."

With a visible wince on her face, Angela stepped over the bottle and made her way over to the Wolf's feet. "Come on. At least let me try face-first."

Drake shook his head. "Honestly, Ann, there's no way in hell you'll get your mouth around those shoulders." I took a chance to ogle Ali's body again. Juxtaposed to her narrow waist, her shoulders looked monolithic. I could understand Drake's point. Feet first, Angela could start thin and work her way up to the thickest part, like putting on a condom, or like how it was always easier for pointy-nosed Furs to get their heads stuck in between banisters than it was to pull them back out.

"Fuck that," Angela said with sharp dismissiveness. "She'll

lock her legs as they slide into my stomach and keep me from swallowing."

Smart Bunny. I had never considered that. I always assumed preds preferred to eat their meals head-first because a prey's head level was closer to the maw, but now that I also thought about how spines curved, it *would* be easier to cram a prey into a tight space like that if forced to curl up.

Angela turned around—her ears whipped to the side—and whined, "Roooooooss!"

Ross, almighty referee, nodded. "Pred gets the choice. Turn around, girl." He cycloned his finger in the air, and with an annoyed grimace, Ali rocked forwards and perched up on her knees.

"Don't choke," Ali grunted as the Bunny closed the distance. As Angela hesitated, I caught the double meaning of that.

My tail thumped on the floor as I watched with rapt interest. All of this was because I wanted to get lucky with a girl, and even though she clearly wasn't interested in me, it would be insult to injury if we were stuck playing this while she was in some Bunny's stomach.

Everyone was engaged with varying degrees of interest. I almost expected a betting pool to break out, but then again, in a game where lives were on the line, what else could possibly be gambled? Angela opened her mouth as wide as she could and lowered herself awkwardly over Ali's head. I couldn't help it. Ali was so gorgeous that seeing her stunning head disappear into someone else's mouth made me utter what could only be characterized as a squeak. Fuck me; I was an idiot. The Hyena across the circle noticed my little yelp and rolled her eyes and shook her head. I wished I could be as calm as her. Amber, I think her name was, looked away, disinterested, like she already knew the outcome. The Hyena leaned back to support her weight on a palm and then inspected the shiny umber claws of her other paw. I bet she could take on Ali no problem. She was a bit taller than the Wolf and she had a certain amount of thickness from nose to toes. Maybe she ate people even more often than Ali did, or maybe Ali worked out a lot more between prey to keep that figure.

Speaking of Ali, she was literally in the process of being eaten. I turned my attention back to that and watched as Angela's cheeks puffed out. The She-Wolf's head was gone. The Bunny groped Ali's shoulders and tried to push herself farther down like Abe had to that Fennec. Her lips only stretched about halfway down the wide slope of Ali's shoulders before plateauing. Angela strained to stretch wider, but she couldn't. She could only extend her jaws in the other direction. She tried twisting herself to eat the Wolf sideways, but that proved just as awkward. Drake chuckled.

Angela's eyes winced shut as she started to flush with embarrassment. I heard straining noises from her. Or I *thought* she was making straining noises until I detected a melody to them. That was when I realized the sound was in fact humming from the head inside her muzzle. My jaw dropped. Ali was humming the goddamn theme from *Jeopardy*. When others caught on, the whole circle—not counting Tailor and me—started cackling. This circle of shame seemed to only fire up Angela even more. She pushed down with her splayed muzzle and shoved upwards with her paws tight around the Wolf's arms, but it was no use. Finally, Angela pulled up. Ali's head, dripping with drool, was revealed as the Bunny fell back. She worked her locked jaw up and down and side to side. "Fuck. Fuck fuck fuck!" She hammered a dent into the corner of the pizza box with her fist.

Ali shook her head and blinked in the light. "Ross!" She held up her paw. The massive Orca reached behind himself and pulled out an enormous t-shirt. I had to assume it was his. He tossed the blanket-sized article of clothing her way, and she used it to wipe herself clean. Once dried off, Ali shot me a spiteful look. "Told you I'm tough to get down."

I looked at the floor. "I'm sorry for accidentally insinuating I would eat you."

"Yeah. Whatever."

Ross spun the app wheel again. It was Drake's turn, and

everyone immediately went on edge. Even Ali stiffened as he swung the bottle into a spin with his enormous padded paws. Based on the Tiger's size, I knew that this would not be like the last round. Lady luck was a cruel mistress tonight, as the green bottle's nose angled towards Angela.

"Nooooo!" She beat her fists against her forehead. "No no no!"

Bianca shook her head. "That sucks." The Pig didn't actually seem sympathetic. I couldn't really fault her though. Angela's sealed fate guaranteed that I wouldn't be Tiger food tonight, and I was grateful for that.

"Should've spun it just a bit harder on your turn," Ali teased. "You definitely could have eaten this little poser." She shouldered me, and I grunted.

"I'm not a poser."

Tailor spoke up again. "Come on guys. This is horrible!"

"Where was that insight when *my* head was in a mouth?" Ali blasted.

"She's terrified!"

Angela's head was buried in her paws. Her soft lop ears drooped down and veiled her face. Maybe she was praying.

"I'm not terrified," she snapped. The Bunny jerked her head up, and despite the little hints of moisture in her fur in the corners of her eyes, her expression was steeled with resolve. "I'm ready."

"No!" Tailor argued.

The Bunny pointed her paw at my friend. "Stop. This is the way it is. So shut your fucking mouth. This isn't about you. It's about *me*."

"And me," Drake added with a shake of his muscly gut.

"I want this."

"What?" Tailor wasn't alone in his confusion. I was equally aghast.

"Aww, you sap," Drake cooed.

"Shut the fuck up, Stripey." 'Sap' was obviously being used facetiously.

Angela stood up and took a deep breath. She tapped her toes on the carpet, a bit of nervousness she quickly quashed with a full-body shake, and marched across the circle to the other side. Drake bore a satisfied grin. "That's my good girl." He took her by the paw and drew her close. To my surprise, they pressed their mouths together in a kiss that held for several seconds. While my jaw dropped, no one else reacted in the slightest, and I wondered what the hell was going on here. When the kiss separated, Drake smiled. "Always knew it would end like this, didn't ya?"

Angela rolled her eyes. "You've been eyeing me with your stomach since we first banged it out."

"You guys are dating!?" Tailor exclaimed.

"I don't think we need to *label* it," Drake said passively.

"I was hoping you could show me the ropes once I got my first prey," Angela said, cupping the Tiger's cheek. She sighed and addressed the group, but I had a feeling she was more saying this to Tailor. "It's hard for us Bunnies to earn that pred status. This was my chance, and I blew it, so if we can't be preds together, at least I can be prey for someone I care about."

Tailor turned away and buried his face in his palms like he was about to scream. Of course, I didn't even know where my own feelings lied on this issue. Part of me was still coming down from the anxiety spike of the Tiger spinning the bottle. But there was something honest with the Bunny's convictions. This wasn't just pride and accepting one's fate. Now that she'd worked through the initial shock of the bottle deciding her immediate destiny and the cruel irony that she was picked moments after failing to be a pred herself, it really seemed like she wanted this. Maybe it was *because* she couldn't be a pred. It sounded like that was something they actually had wanted to focus the relationship on. This was not something I would have wanted for myself, but I understood the poetry of it all, even if Tailor looked like his brain was about to burst out of his ears.

"Everyone has to make peace with the fact that they could be prey for someone," Amber said with a nod. "I'm proud of you, Ann."

Angela shook her head ruefully. "You're just happy that you didn't get chosen by the one guy in the circle who could swallow you."

The Hyena cupped her paw around air and mimed like she was raising a glass in agreement. "Sassy to the end."

Drake just looked up at the Bunny and smiled. He kept caressing her like he was memorizing her shape. "That's my girl. I'm gonna miss ya."

At that moment, Tailor whipped back around. "Then don't-"

"Owwwwmf!" Drake noisily clamped his jaws around Angela's much smaller head. With his beefy arms, he lifted her upside down and into the air. It only took three powerful gulps to seal her away in his mouth. One final swallow sent the Bunny gliding down his gullet and into his stomach. He leaned back as the smooth orb expanded a bit. The shape didn't betray the prey's form; it was too thick with muscle, but it enlarged a little in all directions, and his shirt rode up a couple inches. "Urrrrrp!" he belched. "Okay. Who's next?"

It was so quick; so casual. The way he patted his stomach as if he had just eaten a cookie and not his... not-girlfriend. I truly wanted to admire Angela. The bottle said, 'Let them eat Bunny,' and she went out head held high like Marie Fucking Antoinette. I'd never seen a prey act like that. It was as if she was *proud* to be Drake's dinner. Usually that was something I'd only seen projected on prey from stuffed predators, an idea that prey should be 'honored' to fulfill their role in the food chain. A platitude. I'd never seen it in practice from the other side though. Then I thought of Max's old roommate. He hadn't been proud to be a meal, and he certainly hadn't stayed in there willingly, but he enjoyed the thrill of it enough to do it for fun if his safety was guaranteed. Maybe Angela enjoyed it on some level, too. *If I survive this, I'll see if Drake will let me ask her how it felt to be eaten through his stomach.* The Tiger belched again, louder this time. *If she's still conscious by the end of the game.*

Once Ross reconfigured the wheel's settings to remove Tiger and Bunny, he spun it again.

Cat.

For some insulting reason I was 'Fatter Cat,' and everyone knew it, so instead we all turned to Tailor, who hadn't looked back at the circle since he closed his eyes during the swallowing of Angela. We all stared at him expectantly.

"Cat," the Mouse parroted.

He didn't respond.

I cleared my throat. "Tailor, it's your turn to spin."

"I'm not playing," he said stiffly. His tail thumped the carpet twice.

"Yes you are," I argued. "We're all playing. Whether we like it or not."

"I'm. Not. Playing."

I was afraid this would happen. His chance of being eaten was the same as mine—he wasn't much skinnier than me. When not worrying about myself, I'd been worried about one of these predators getting him. I didn't think I would have to worry about if he got a chance to eat someone else. "Tailor, don't be a stubborn idiot. This is your out. Spin the bottle, and after your turn, you can leave."

"Not if I have to eat someone."

Everyone groaned. I knew Tailor was stubborn about not ending up as prey. I didn't think he would be the same about being a predator. He seemed to view the whole concept of Predation as some bullshit slippery slope.

"Who brought this stick in the mud?" the Mouse squeaked.

Ali jerked her thumb at me. "Poser here."

"Yeah well *you* brought the poser," Drake pointed out. "*Urrrp.* 'Scuse me. Mmmm. Damn, let's wrap this up. I wanna go find another Bunny before the party's over."

"To fuck or eat?" the Pig snorted.

Drake shrugged.

"Jesus Christ, what is *wrong* with you people!" Tailor shouted.

"Oh for Christ's sake," I exploded. I leaned into the circle and spun it. Three times it went around before ending on the

Mouse. "There. He spun the Mouse. Now just... eat her and go."

The Mouse started to squeak in protest. Ross was quick to call foul and ease her mind, but Tailor and I were still arguing.

"I'm not going to be a predator. I'm not like these people, okay? I'm not like *you*."

"Oh my God, I'm so sick of your self-righteous bullshit!" I yelled.

"I'm not doing it! I never have, and I never will, so stop it!"

"I'm trying to save your life, stupid! You're the one who's been bitching the whole time. She's just a fucking Mouse!"

"Can we have respect for the Mouse?" the Mouse queried.

"Agreed. We may be eating each other, but we can still have basic respect," Ross chastised.

"Agh!" Tailor's claws were out as he raked the fur on his head. He then pointed at me. "This is all your fault. You talk about gay people being too sexual, but you're the thirsty slut who walked us into a death match to get some tail!"

Ali folded her arms. "The Tail has a name."

"So does the Mouse," the Mouse piped in again.

"*Urrrrrrp,*" Drake belched. "This stress is bad for my digestion."

"I'm trying to help you!" I yelled.

"Don't give me that. This is all your fault we got roped into this! I didn't even want to come here tonight!"

"I didn't want you to come either! I wish you hadn't!"

"I wish I hadn't too! I guess I'm just a better person than you are!"

"I guess you fucking are then!"

We breathed heavily at each other. The whole circle went silent. The only sound in the nook was the chime of a cell phone. Everyone looked towards Ross. "Wolf," he announced.

"What? No! It's still Tailor's turn."

"If he's not going to play," Ross said rather bored, "then his turn is over. Wolf."

Ali sat up. "About damn time." She spun the bottle with ferocity. It went around once, twice, thrice... frourice? On the fifth turn it ended on the Mouse.

"Fuck!" she shouted.

I stared at the floor. Tailor and I both did. A few articles of clothing flew across the room as Ali made quick work of her meal... whatever her name was. Big Bad Ali sat back, picking shredded blouse out of her teeth and rubbing the lump in her tum.

"Come on, Ross," Bianca badgered. "Pick me before all the small prey are taken."

"I am bound by the wheel," he said with practiced apathy.

The Pig folded her arms. "Round as one too."

"Want *me* to eat you?"

"Hmph."

The phone chimed, and Ross groaned. "Fatter Cat."

My ears perked up. I was still in a mode of fury, and the first thing out of my mouth was, "You couldn't just label me 'Tabby Cat' or... just asked names?" The Orca shrugged with indifference. To be fair, I wasn't this group's favorite person— probably not their *least* favorite given Tailor's current attitude— but I was up there... down there. Whatever; fuck it. It was my turn to finally try Predation, and I was nice and pissed off. I didn't care that it would upset Tailor. He had his chance to nut up and leave us in peace, but he had to be a stubborn ass about it.

I looked around. I didn't like my prospects. Ali had been too tough for the Rabbit, and while I was bigger than she had been, I still doubted I'd fair much better. The Hyena girl, Amber, was even stockier. That meant the Pig was my only sure shot. I took a breath. "And I'm not fat."

"I said fatter," Ross corrected.

"It's muscle!"

"Spin the bottle, Poser," Ali chided while stifling a burp. Despite the big globe of distended stomach hanging out under the hem of her belly shirt, I suspected the Mouse hadn't been as filling as she had wanted. Given her earlier brags, I bet she wouldn't hesitate to tuck me in there with her other prey if I caused trouble; though, I was more likely to get gobbled up by our voracious referee.

Not wanting to waste any more time, I spun it as hard as I could. It whirled around as a smear of green. The lip of the bottle whistled as it went around and around. I lost track of how many times. When it finally began to slow down, it passed the Pig and arced towards Amber. *Shit shit.* It passed her then arced back around again. It passed me *and* Bianca. Then finally it stalled. The bottle pointed halfway between Tailor and the Hyena.

Everyone looked down at the bottle and then up at Ross.

"Re-spin?" I asked.

Ross looked down at the bottle. His dark eyes squinted, and he stroked his chin. As if that would somehow change things, he tilted his head. "Hmmmm." Everyone was tense. Then Ross decided. "Cat."

As Amber casually slumped into a relaxed state, Tailor froze.

"What? But it's in the middle!" I cried.

Ross squinted again. "Nope. Just *sliiiightly* angled towards the *Cat.*" He said 'Cat' with unfiltered contempt.

"But-"

"Referee!" he shouted. Not a very unbiased one.

Tailor and I locked eyes. "Chance, you have to forfeit!"

I gulped.

Ali coughed, "Poser," and the itch to my pride flared up. I leered at her briefly and then turned my attention back to Tailor.

"I can't eat him. He's my roommate!"

Drake snorted. "I ate my girl."

"And I ate my friend," Abe added with a pat to his stomach. "That's the game."

"Forfeit, Chance," Tailor pleaded.

"I... I..."

Ross leaned forwards and raised the phone, threatening to spin the wheel again. I'd been really lucky so far. There were still four of us left though. If I forfeited there was a fifty percent chance the next person would be Tailor or me again. Which meant there was also a fifty percent chance the wheel would select the Hyena or the Pig. And then there was a... *Fuck! Why was I so bad at math?* Sixty-six. Oh God. If one of those two got a turn, there would be a whopping sixty-six percent chance that Tailor or I would be screwed on that bottle spin and eaten. The Hyena would have no trouble with any of us; I knew that for sure. She had a soft enough tummy that would stretch around a Cat. That Pig Bianca was about my size, but she was... for lack of a better word... porky, and Tailor and I were thin... well thinner. She would have a good enough chance at getting us down that I had to consider her a viable threat.

"I..."

I appraised Tailor. All I had to do was eat him, and I'd get the out that he'd thrown away. *No. No. It's Tailor.* God, I was so mad at him. Fuck him. I hated him right now for being such a dick. But he was still Tailor.

I needed to forfeit. If I was lucky, the Pig and the Hyena would get each other, and we'd be the only ones left. We could 'win' by stalemate. Then I remembered what the Pig said about running out of small prey. Bianca was aware of her limitations. She wouldn't be able to swallow Amber. The circle had unanimously implied only Drake would have had the skill and size to eat her. So, assuming Ross picked Bianca next, and she spun Amber, the game wouldn't end. Bianca getting chosen would yield a one in three chance of prolonging this all another round and a two in three chance of her trying (and quite possibly succeeding) to eat Tailor or me.

We could only guarantee the stalemate if the Hyena was next *and* she lucked onto the Pig. What was thirty-three percent of twenty-five percent? That was our odds of survival. Was that even how math worked? Tailor and his love of statistics would know. That nerd. *Fuck him. Fuck Tailor.* He could have ended this last round by eating someone. Then I wouldn't be in this situation. I could have had the Pig or tried the Hyena. I would have rather tried and failed to eat Amber than throw my shot away like Tailor did. He even got the Mouse. What a waste of the easy prey! What kind of Cat *was* he?

Ali started humming *Jeopardy* again.

"Shut up!"

Tailor just stared at me in horror. He blinked stupidly. "Chance?" It was barely a gasp. A wheeze of fear.

"I'm trying to do math here!" I snapped. Fuck it. The math didn't even matter. What difference did it make how good or bad the odds were? As long as there was a chance I could end up in a belly, I couldn't risk it. There was only one sure thing. Here and now.

"Tailor... come here."

"No." His voice was small and weak, unbelieving.

"Come here, Tailor," I said again.

The smaller Cat shook his head. His eyes were like little emerald saucers, worming their way into my mind with guilt. I squashed it down the best I could.

"I want him head-first," I announced. I wanted to hide those eyes from view as quickly as possible.

"Chance, you can't!"

Amber grasped Tailor's shoulder. The moment her large paw settled on him his whole body tensed, and he tried to make a break for it. Scrabbling backwards, he nearly got to his feet, but the tough Hyena lurched forwards and pinned him.

"Agh! Get off me! Get *off* me!"

Amber was clearly experienced with subduing prey, and she managed to flip him over onto his stomach, stuff her paws under his armpits, and twist back. Picking him up by his armpits, she got up and carried the small feline across the circle like he was a very obstinate sack of potatoes. Amber waddled over and grunted, "Figured he'd need some *encouragement*." A slick grin split her muzzle.

Tailor kicked and flailed. "No! No no no no no!" Louder and louder he yelled, like a kid who thought volume equaled persuasion. It was unbearable as he thrashed his head from side to side. I just wanted it to stop.

I stood up to my full height, clapped my paws against his cheeks, fingers gripping the back curves of his jaw bone, and stuffed his head into my mouth. His protests were instantly muffled as I crammed my tongue up against his face, and the screaming was replaced with hearty cheers.

"Thank God," Abe breathed from his corner. Everyone on the floor sat back and displayed equal signs of relief, like when the residence hall fire drill ended and the piercing wails of the alarm finally stopped making our ears bleed. It was the kind of quiet you could appreciate. But while everyone else relaxed, Tailor and I held tension in our full bodies, and I was convinced that we could feel each others' stress, with my mouth as the conduit.

I had my roommate's head in my mouth. I froze. Tailor froze. My heart drummed with the tempo of a bucket-pounding street musician. It was like being 'touched' for the first time, like the break of virginity, but even though I hadn't gone through with it yet, I had the taste on my tongue, and synapses I didn't know I had were connecting in new ways amidst this transition in my life: from non-pred to pred. Wires inside me sent new chemicals and sparks of feeling between my brain, paws, and stomach. I walked my fingertips down the sides of Tailor's neck and held his shoulders, feeling the wound-up muscles beneath his soft short fur. I flexed my fingers possessively.

With an exhale, my body started to relax, just like what those first less-helpful internet recommendations suggested. I inhaled, and his musky scent flared into my nostrils. Whenever I used to walk into our dorm room, if he wasn't there, I could tell how long it had been since he left. Living next to someone made their scent so familiar that if push came to shove, you could pick it out of a crowd. And now that I had his flavor on my tongue, that familiarity satisfied an unspoken longing. It was like having a crush on someone and finally snagging that first kiss. *I swear to God I'm straight*. It was a release as much as a lurch and spike in desire, and the only thought in my head was, *Why haven't I been doing this all along?*

This sudden change, it was crazy. I mean, I'd *licked* people before—throatilingus was a hell of a turn on—but I'd never felt a reaction like this: a desire to push him deeper. There was an ache in my gut, a hole that needed filling, and as I sucked on Tailor's head, and drool started to accumulate in my mouth as if I was a damn Dog, I knew there was only one direction to take this: forward. I looked down my stout snout to see the expanse of his shoulders quivering beneath his shirt.

It was a nice shirt.

It had to go.

I extended my claws and gripped the fabric along his spine and ripped. Just like that, the calm before the storm broke, and Tailor began to panic in earnest. He pushed against me, and I had to pin his arms back down to his sides. Amber had let go, leaving me on my own to finish the deed myself. The taste was unlike anything I'd ever experienced before. On the surface was the scented flavor of perfumed sweat. That musk added a savory sensation to the sweetness of his cologne and the saltiness of his stress-induced perspiration. And by God, I wanted that shirt gone; I wanted to taste all of him going down. I glowered at it and flicked my ears to the Hyena. With a wry grin, she obliged and wrapped her thick fingers around the slight tear in the fabric I'd managed. While I held my roommate as still as I could, she ripped apart the shirt in strips. Tailor thrashed as his t-shirt was torn into pieces. They dangled over my paws where they viced around his biceps.

I remembered what I read earlier and what I saw tonight. Prey struggling was just a part of the process. I took a deep breath through my nose. I had to be careful with my teeth while Tailor tried desperately to yank himself out of my mouth. I didn't want him to hurt himself. That would just ruin this for everyone. Instead I imagined I was sucking on an enormous furry lollipop, letting the internal pressure of the suction hold on rather than exhaust myself with my jaw muscles. That was probably *one* of the places where that Bunny went wrong.

Focus on the flavor, I told myself. There were sandalwood undertones to his cologne. I pictured my roommate as a tropical feast and projected myself on a beach. I needed to stay relaxed. Everything about this was new and almost impossible to compare with anything I had done before. Eventually even the sex metaphors collapsed. The sudden click and shift in my attitudes matched the analogy, but to be honest, this was nothing like the steamy taste of a kiss or something else farther south of the border. Instead, it provided a new outlook on flavor: the taste of Cat. It was good. No wonder Ali wanted me to join the game. If I was half as delicious as Tailor, I wouldn't have been able to blame her for only wanting me as a meal.

At some point I must have closed my eyes in the euphoric bliss of flavor and control. When I opened them, Amber still stood in front of me. Her arms were crossed, and her head was tilted to the side, and she wore a rueful but impressed grin. "You going to eat the rest of him, or you just after some head?"

My ears flattened in embarrassment, and despite the hit it would have brought to my reputation as a straight guy, had my mouth not been full I would have cheekily said, 'It's good head.' Instead I let out my breath through my nose, watching as my steamy exhale stirred Tailor's neck fur. His hackles lifted right up. With every wrenching twist of his neck to try and break free, my tongue, now exploring on its own instinctive accord, probed the nook beneath his jawline. It curled against the ridge of the bone and hooked in with a curl. I shuddered as I felt my own throat open up, prepping for the next step. It felt so natural. I had already crossed a threshold, but once I gulped, there was no going back. This was Tailor. Tailor who came here to keep me safe. But also Tailor who damned me to this decision by not having the guts to do what I was willing to. I always had to choose the hard thing. He always got to stand by his convictions because he was privileged enough to do so. I wasn't. I wasn't some prey waiting to be eaten. I was a predator. I seized the chances that came my way.

I hunched my shoulders and forced my maw down on him. His squat face pushed towards the back of my throat, and when it nudged my pesky uvula, my chest convulsed under the triggering nudge, but I clenched everything and held firm. I crammed him past it and down as my lips splayed across the widening expanse

94

of his shoulders. A skinny twink like Tailor felt a lot thicker in my mouth—that was a bad way to phrase it—than I would have expected, but I knew this would be hard. The challenge was part of the pleasure.

I tried not to get distracted and did what the forums suggested. I focused on his taste. He was food, and delicious food at that. As long as that was in my mind, the overwhelming size of him would be easier to mitigate. Predation was as much a mental thing as a physical thing. I thought about my stomach and the hunger that had started to flare. I pictured Tailor already curled up in there, and imagining the task already being completed helped me relax. I don't put stock into the whole 'if you can visualize it you can make it happen' bullshit, but projecting myself there kept me calm, and that was key.

Lead with the cheeks, I repeated to myself. I already had my jaw lowered enough for his depth, I just needed more horizontal width for those shoulders. I spread my cheeks apart and focused only on that, and little by little my lips inched down the slope of his narrow shoulders. I was more than halfway there. *I got this. I got this!*

The following sudden *clack* in my mandible brought tears to my eyes and made my whole body jolt. My jaw unhinged. *Fuck fuck fuck.* I halted everything. People said this could happen. *Oh shit.* Tailor tried to pull out, and I didn't have any muscular pressure in my mouth to keep him where he was. Just my arms and my back, and both were straining against him. *Dammit Tailor, stop!* Why couldn't he just let me have this! *Let me have you!* This was the only use he could be for me now. He'd damned me to this unfortunate timeline. He owed me. I deserved this! I thought about all the niggles and nuisances.

The way he insulted my intelligence and size and strength. The way he kept me up late at night with his fucking reading lamp. The way he nagged me if even one stray sock of mine inched to his side of the room. Bragging about all those fucking A's he got on his tests. *Looks like all that smarts didn't help you after all, huh?* I didn't just deserve to eat him. *He* deserved to be my food.

I took another deep breath and ignored my unhinged jaw. I'd just have to pop the sucker back into place afterwards. I still had my tongue, and it wasn't strong, but I could use it to my advantage. I stretched my tongue outward as far as I could beyond my lower lip. It lapped the cleft of his pecs and offered me a new flavor. It was crisper, richer. I moaned. I couldn't help it. The taste was so good, and the yearning to get my tongue on more of his body—*How did all of these other preds eat prey of the same gender without constantly feeling gay?*—helped me get another inch downward. Then I noticed something else. When I moaned, he winced. His whole body twisted in disgust. I could feel the grimace of his face against the back of my throat, and I wanted to just push that face deeper, bury it in flesh. My paws slid down to his wrists and crammed upwards, and with just a twinge of aching stretch, I had him.

I could barely feel his shape in my strained mouth, but my tongue pressed deeper along the groove of his chest, and when I opened my eyes, I saw that I had his shoulders. My tail flicked back and forth in excitement. I did it. And the others seemed to recognize it too. As my eyes darted around, Amber gave me a thumbs up and a faint smile. A couple of the others had scooted around the circle to get a better view. Drake, with his own full stomach, drummed his fingers on the expanded curve straining his shirt. I wanted to have a full belly like that. He looked so comfy with his girl wriggling inside of him.

"He's doing it, Ange," he said rather loudly so his meal could hear. "Wish you were out here to see it. If he'd gone first, he might have been able to show you how a little guy does it."

If my jaw was working, I would have smirked. For the first time that day, with what seemed like constant digs at my height, I felt validated. My size was just a property, not a liability, not something to mock, or a reason to doubt me. Maybe I could usher in a new age of small preds finally getting their chance to feel as amazing as I currently felt.

Ali glared at the Tiger. "Are you saying you would have liked to see me get eaten by a Bunny."

"Yeah," Drake barked. "That woulda been ironic as hell."

"Not technically ironic," the Pig pointed out, "But yeah, it would've been pretty funny."

The brown Wolf crossed her arms and looked away, not indulging in me as the others were, but that didn't bother me. She was just bitter that she hadn't gotten to eat one of the two Cats that she'd invited.

Bianca stood up and circled around me with a wrinkled muzzle, critical of my technique. "Hmm. Oof. Looks like his jaw came out, but he's got it so far. As long as he doesn't choke. Metaphorically... literally too."

Even Ross sat up and half-smiled. And that fueled me. I liked encouragement. It was something I never got from stupid Tailor. Thinking about how little he supported me all the time gave me the fire to stuff him deeper into my mouth. But then I slowed down. This was still my first time, and I wanted to enjoy it, and the others who remained in the circle seemed to accept that and didn't give me a hard time.

With the biggest hurdle over, I surrendered myself solely to the pleasure. Tailor must have known how far my mouth had stretched over his shoulders, and he tried to wriggle harder to get out, but I kept bearing down on him. My grip on his arms was steel. It had to be. If he so much as raised his arms, he might have been able to pop himself back out. Not only would my turn be over and I'd have to risk being a meal for the Pig or the Hyena, but even if everything went perfectly in our favor, and we could both walk out of here with the Pig gurgling away into Hyena fat, we wouldn't be able to just go back to our dorm room together. There was no turning back from this.

I forced my head down farther. His burgeoning deltoids filled out my cheeks as the lower swells of his pecs grooved along my tongue like a bum on a bicycle seat. I slathered him with saliva to make him slicker and also keep his flavor fresh on my tongue. I stepped back to reduce the angle of my throat, and for a split moment, I ran the risk of him getting free, but I held strong.

It was time for the first swallow. And it was good. My throat was like one of those squishy snake water-wiggler things that fold in on themselves and fly out of your paw... except reverse. It rolled around his head and embraced him. I could feel the fullness under my chin as I worked down his chest. I didn't want to lose the momentum, so I swallowed again. My throat proved to be the most effective tool. Instinct took over, and I trusted my innate bodily mechanics. This was survival of the fittest, the hungriest, and those willing to take.

And by God did Tailor taste delicious. My undulating throat quickly caught a rhythm with my arms shoving him into me, and before I knew it, I was at his navel. My tongue slipped right into the tiny divot hiding in his fluffy midriff. The flavor was even richer in there. It was concentrated with sweat and musk and all the natural flavors of a Cat.

And as his tail flicked about fruitlessly, I couldn't help but snort. If Tailor knew how yummy he was, he probably would have seen my side of this more. With him this far in, I didn't need to pin his arms down anymore, and the shreds of his shirt piled at our feet, so I seized his tail and tugged on it playfully. It gave him a little jolt that caused him to lurch himself deeper down my gullet. This disrupted the rhythm, but it was funny and brought as much of a smile to my stretched out, jaw-dislocated muzzle as possible. Maybe fooling around was cocky, but Tailor was just rump and legs now.

Part of me got a little curious—after all, I already had literal man in my mouth—to strip him for all he was worth and steal the flavor of those meaty thighs we'd been strength training together, but a cock on my tongue was more than I was willing to do even for something as innocuous as Predation. I'd definitely have to ask Max some advice for getting over that hurdle given he ate a fully naked dude in the shower this morning. Plus, I didn't want to waste too much time. His upper half had plumped out my throat and chest. Muscles strained. It was tough to breathe. My ribs felt tight with him in me, and I wanted to put him where he belonged.

I grabbed both his thighs in my paws and tried to lift him up. It was hard, and I almost lost my balance, but I managed to upend him. Teetering on unstable legs, I turned awkwardly towards the circle of predators as he started sliding in faster. Tailor's pants didn't taste that great, as expected, but the sensation of stuffing myself made up for the dry feeling of denim on my tongue. Every gulp worked him farther down. Once it was just his calves sticking comically out of my mouth, I took the time to stroke the bulge in my throat. My fingers danced over the firmness of body just below the softness of my skin pulled so tautly. Roving down the front of my body, my paws caressed my stomach. I could feel his head slipping into it, and I wanted to feel it fill out all the way. I plopped down hard on one of the pillows on the floor and the plummeting jerk of my body mixed with gravity pulled in my roommate the rest of the way.

His feet went over my tongue and disappeared down the void of my throat, and the huge hulking weight of another Anthro nearly my size spilling into my gut was the best feeling I'd ever experienced. The sudden expansion stretched my shirt to its breaking point. *Shit.* I forgot to unbutton beforehand. There was a sound of ripping fabric, and then buttons bulleted across the nook. Bianca shielded herself with her arms. One of the buttons bounced right off of Ross's massive belly. I blushed, but I couldn't apologize. The shape of my expanding furry stomach stretching out in front of me stole all of my attention. All I could do was bust out a low huff of exertion. I took some deep breaths as all the stretched-out parts above my belly receded back to their normal size. My gut, though, was staggering.

While obviously not as bulky, I had a body similar to the Tiger's, so my tight muscular gut didn't give way that much as far as shapeliness, but like Drake's it grew exorbitantly like an airbag. Everything was stretched so thin I thought I might pop if I was so much as pricked with a claw. I rubbed over my huge round stomach as it ballooned and smothered my entire lap. If I pressed on it enough with my palm I could feel the curves of Tailor's body inside of me. I tried to voice my own surreal feelings, but it only came out as a clumsy garble. I forgot that my jaw was still unhinged, and it flopped grossly. This was gonna hurt. With a preemptive wince, I seized it and snapped it back into place, and the sharp sting that lurched through my body provoked a yowl of pain. Barely a moment had passed when a pressure surged up my gullet, and I thought I would hurl, but when my mouth puffed open of its own accord, I was pleased to hear only a long loud belch.

I covered my muzzle out of habit, and the other people chuckled at my resulting blush. I had almost forgotten I wasn't alone. All of their eyes were on me, waiting for me to say something. I had trouble finding the words. I felt so full and satisfied.

Inside my huge stomach, Tailor twitched and wriggled. With us practically being the same size, my belly was much too tight for him to push out with any of his limbs like what I often saw with bigger and pudgier predators, like I'd seen from Ross when we passed him on our way here. My whole gut just wobbled back and forth like an indecisive Pokéball. *Shit. Tailor's nerdiness was rubbing off on me.* Hopefully, unlike the balls in that stupid app, I wouldn't explode without warning. As the sharp edges of elbows and heels chafed against the inner walls, and nothing seemed to be breaking, calmness started to settle.

I released a huff of tensed breath and cracked a grin. "Alright *now* you can call me the Fatter Cat."

With the enormous caramel globe of body rising up in front of me, I could only imagine how much weight I was going to gain from this ordeal. Though I had already made peace with it when I decided to become a Predator, I still felt a twinge of regret that Tailor was going to absolutely wreck my developing abs that I'd been working so hard towards. It would be a big shift to get used to. On the other paw, a bunch of the other preds here were pretty fit like Ali and Abe, so maybe they would have some pointers.

The Hyena sat back down next to me. "Alright, so... I think we know how this ends," she said pointing her finger between the Pig and herself and back again. "Can we just do this."

"No!" The Pig cried more indignant than fearful. "I at least get a *chance!*"

I sat back as my shifting gut full of Cat made muffled sounds of distress. I was so absorbed in my own body I could barely care what happened next. No wonder Abe had been so quiet for most of the game. Honestly, *everyone* was preoccupied with their big bellies now. I supposed once you sealed someone away in your gut it was hard to focus on anyone else. While I marveled at the immense size of my midsection and tended to the growing ache of tightness by rubbing it in soothing circles, Ross spun the wheel on which only two colors remained. I wasn't engrossed by any means, but out of the corner of my eye, I saw that Amber won. Not even bothering to spin the bottle since no matter where it pointed, it would be closest to the Pig, the Hyena pounced across the circle and greedily scarfed up her prey feet first—a bold and confident move.

I looked up from my own stomach to watch. Amber teasingly dug her teeth into the Pig's flabby belly just enough to play with the fleshy softness. Inch by inch Bianca disappeared. The Pig grimaced the whole way down until jaws clamped over her head. The Hyena sat back as her belly swelled out. It was quick work, economical. I could tell Amber had enjoyed herself, but the speed bespoke practiced skill, and she seemed more interested in the final result than the process. Once her stomach settled, she patted the engorged dome and burped. The Pig's glasses, covered with slime, spewed out on the burst of expelled air, and we laughed.

Ross flopped back on his side and slipped his phone back into his cargo pants pockets. "Alright, we are *done.*" He seemed relieved, which was fair. I bet none of them had expected such an ordeal from tonight, and I couldn't help but feel self-conscious about it. No one said anything though.

Drake stood up first. "I'm gonna take my girl home. I wanna enjoy this before the squirming stops, if you know what I mean." I think I partly understood what he meant, but who was to say? *What a complicated relationship.* I watched him go while his white and black striped tail lashed back and forth. Abe got up next and stumbled off without a word. He just waved over his shoulder. He still looked a bit drunkenly loopy even with such a big meal in him. I imagined he'd be passed out somewhere downstairs within a few minutes.

The others all stayed put.

"Ugh, I always get the fat ones," Amber griped. "I was just starting to work off the weight from my last prey too."

Ali snorted laughter. "I'd trade you if I could. That Mouse wasn't filling at all."

I tilted my head at Ali and wondered how eating anything that could swell your belly to the size of an exercise ball could be categorized as 'not filling.' But by comparison alone I understood that there was a difference. Looking down, my own body resembled an exercise ball hanging off my abdomen. With Ali's broad upper body, the distended lump in her stomach hardly looked as awkward as most predators did after a meal *du Anthro*. The Mouse could be seen squirming through her creamy belly fur. Had Ali worn a full-length shirt, she could have passed for just stuffing a plush toy in there.

"I was hoping for something more," and the brown Wolf looked directly at me. I gulped.

Amber shook her head. "You just love your 'Three Little Pigs' fantasy."

"One day I *will* get three at once."

"God, I would kill for your metabolism."

"Oh shut up. You got curves. Own it. Plus, with a body like that, it's gotta be easy to keep men in line."

Deciding to hop in, I added, "It'd work on me."

"Nah," she said flippantly. "Guys are lame; they never wanna date preds. You know how they are with their fragile masculinity and all. Always afraid we'll be bigger and tougher than them."

"And eat them," Ali pointed out.

The Hyena burped again and shrugged. Then she cocked her head towards me. "How about it, 'straight boy?' You ever date a pred?"

My minimal experience with girls got caught in my throat as easily as Tailor's shoulders had. "W-well-" I rubbed the back of my head. "I *haven't*, but I *would*."

"Yeah that's what they always say." Ali leaned back against the wall.

"I mean it. I... just haven't dated much in general. High school I was always busy working and shit. But I wouldn't say no to the concept, and you can trust me on that." I trained my gaze onto Ali's face. Maintaining steely eye contact, I rubbed my stomach for emphasis. "I'm not a poser."

The She-Wolf stroked her chin in slow consideration and then snorted. "Yeah. I suppose you aren't." All predators had a limit of what they were able to stomach, and that concession seemed to be the most that Ali could admit, and while I stopped caring about her and the attentions that had lured me up to this nook in the first place, there was a certain satisfaction in earning her begrudging respect in front of the remaining preds.

With a snorting pout, she pressed down on her stomach, cramming her prey deeper into whatever gunk would have been sloshing around in there. The squelch was audible even over the constant din of partiers echoing up from the first floor.

Meanwhile Tailor kept rocking back and forth in his own limited space. His occasional jabs at my virgin belly made me wince. *Bony little fucker.* I crossed my arms, resting them on what was probably my ex-roommate's head. It was such a strange and uncanny thing to see myself blimped out like this, and yet it felt right. All my life I'd wanted to feel powerful, and as Tailor wriggled as best he could in my cramped stomach, I finally felt that power I'd always desired. I rubbed my paw over the huge furry dome. I should have felt guilty, but I just didn't. It felt too natural to be wrong. Sitting among these preds and shooting the shit while our meals digested? It was like when my dad went out for drinks with the other fishermen. Or when Tailor went to his pretentious coffee shops to talk about stodgy old literature or whatever. These were my people. Tailor was my meal. It was a perfect fit. Literally.

"So... I assume this was your first time predding?" Amber asked.

"Well yeah... but there's a first time for everything right?" I belched and a hint Tailor's flavor wafted under my nose. *What a taste.* I sighed, content, but then the resulting quiet started to build uncomfortably like a stubborn burp. I cleared my throat with a cough and said, "I'm... sorry for all the trouble this guy caused." I smacked my gut and watched it wobble. "Prey guys, ya know?"

"It'll be good to see him as fat," Ross rumbled from his spot on the couch. "Annoying little tits. It's one thing to raise a stink about not wanting to be eaten. *No one* wants that-"

"I wouldn't say that," I interrupted, thinking about Max's Predation video. "I knew a guy who was really into it actually. Of course, he never wanted to be gurgled up, and he really put up a fight when his pred started to digest him."

"Yeah. Some folks like the nice cozy squish." He patted his belly and it jiggled. "I've downed a few willing prey myself, but they always want it to be safe. Real world ain't safe though."

"Exactly," I agreed. It was like I was finally talking to people who understood.

Ali nodded. "It pisses *me* off when people go out of their way to talk about *not* eating Anthros. What do they think announcing that to the room is gonna get them laid? All he had to do was eat a Mouse!" She glanced down at her belly with disappointment. I knew that look. It was the look when all the millennials got out of college and thought life was gonna be good, when you wanted a lot and got saddled with significantly less. "Hope you enjoyed him," she spat at me. "He cost me a much better meal."

"Aww, wanna trade?" Amber teased. She rubbed her big belly, flaunting her fullness.

"Hmph."

Ali looked away, but I couldn't help but catch eyes with the Hyena. We exchanged smiles. Her hair was cropped and punky, a rich dark umber. Her big chocolate brown eyes blended into her pupils, so her expression was bit hard to read, but it seemed welcoming. She was a little chubby from neck to toe, but I didn't mind that. She bore the curves well as Ali had pointed out. With prey in her belly, her midriff swelled forwards. Her love handles framed the shape that spilled past the hem of her own belly shirt, and it looked like a scoop of chocolate ice cream. The swells that rose and fell in her belly were subtle under the softer flab, and I also had the feeling that her own prey was much more accepting of her fate than mine was. There were no jolts or jabs. The motions were smooth, as if Bianca was just trying to get comfortable in her new home.

"May I?" I asked nodding at her stomach.

Amber scooted to the side and relaxed against the foot of the couch. Then she opened her paws palm out to me, with her stomach between them.

Scooting on my butt with my big belly like a ball and chain in my lap, I settled down next to her. I hesitated for a moment with my paw over her stomach. I'd been around predators before. I'd slapped a full belly now and then, usually with jest rather than admiration. I touched her soft flesh and dug my fingers into the squish. I couldn't help it. I shuddered. I could feel Bianca's harder features deep inside if I pressed down, like when you lose your phone in bed and find it under the pillow, the brick under the plush. A smile curled up my muzzle.

"Soft huh?" she asked.

I nodded.

"Yeah. I'm a chunky gal."

"I'm a short dude."

"Aww." She put her arm around me, a sign of solidarity. "Look at the two of us disappointing western beauty standards together."

I knew she was kidding around, but she kept the arm there and leaned into the contact. Ross rolled his eyes. "Oh, such trailblazers." I supposed a five hundred pound Orca could recognize the first-world problems of our self-image dilemmas, and we laughed. We were all in on the joke though. "No one's giving *me* affection," he grumbled in what I guessed was mock disappointment.

"Ross," Ali said pointedly, "It's not because you're fat as fuck that no one wants to sleep with you. It's because you could eat a whole damn orgy."

"Otherwise you'd be riding this dick?" he asked hopefully.

"Maybe when I *know* you're full."

"Quick!" He gestured towards himself urgently with one big hand. "Someone bring me one more Fur. My sex life is on the line. Amber. Pass me the fat Cat."

The hair on my hackles rose. I couldn't be one hundred percent sure if he was kidding, but Amber just curled her paw tighter around my shoulders. "Sorry. I'm using him right now."

"Do I give a good belly rub?" I asked, kneading a little bit more until my fingers started to massage the Pig inside.

Both Amber and her meal settled into my touch. "Good enough. I'll have to give you some pointers since you're new to this circle."

My heart pounded as a lurid idea crept into my mind. It would be my second risk tonight to get with someone, but since there was clearly nothing but hunger for me from Ali, I might as well toss my net somewhere else. "Now when you say 'circle,'" I drawled carefully. "Do you mean this little social group... or this beautiful pork-stuffed belly?" And to punctuate my flirtation I reached over with my other paw and cupped the supple squish of her stomach.

Amber appraised me with a wry grin and turned her attention towards the others in the nook. "I like him."

"Dammit," Ross muttered. "Ali, can you bring me up a snack? Really don't care who."

"Don't you have a whole house of brothers at your beck and call?"

I jerked my head towards the Orca. "You're Gamma Upsilon Tau?"

He winked. "President."

Holy shit. That was why his name sounded familiar. He was the Ross that Max had mentioned earlier. I'd been so preoccupied all night with getting some Predation experience, I almost forgot I'd wanted to also try and schmooze a few of the brothers here to get on their radar. I chewed on my lip, though, also remembering that Max had told me to watch out for him specifically. Of course, if I could get in with Ross, that could also be a huge leg up to getting into this frat next year. I'd just have to make sure that 'in with Ross' only extended to the societal metaphor and nothing literal. He seemed like the kind of guy who would and could eat anyone. Then again, he had displayed a hell of a lot of emphasis on things like fairness tonight. On one paw, he implied that everyone he added to his gut wasn't personal. On the other, I actually felt like I could trust him... as long as I kept out of scarfing range.

"Well then. Since you're the person to thank for this killer party, I could go down and get someone for ya. What do you like? Bunnies, Foxes, reptiles?"

"Oh, he can get his own food," Amber said waving her paw. "He's had *no* trouble doing it all night."

"That was four Anthros ago," Ross complained. "But fine. I guess it would help to get this fat ass off the couch." Ross chuckled and sat up. He rested his big hands on his knees. His huge stomach shifted across his lap with a *blorp* and a *slosh*. He rubbed the flabby wall of belly that went from neck to knees. It looked soft and big enough that if I ran at it, I'd squelch into its folds and get lost. He hefted himself to his feet and the couch seemed to sigh in relief. He took a moment to arch his back, stretching away the kinks from lying on his side for so long. A loud belch rippled from his mighty jaws, and when it wafted down towards me, I smelled Monkey, Wolf, some kind of lizard, and if I wasn't mistaken, a feline not unlike myself and my own prey. It was practically an Anthro salad in there.

I glanced down at my own stomach, the smile waning from my face. I moved my paws to myself and cradled the angry wriggling lump inside.

"Feeling guilty?" Amber asked. She looked at me seriously. Tailor was still kicking up a storm. It didn't hurt; he didn't have the space to wind up any of his kicks or punches. When Amber's eyes dropped to my gut, I knew what she was thinking. It wasn't too late to let him out. The game was over, and now I could frankly do whatever I wanted. I considered it for a moment. What would I even say to Tailor? "I was just doing it to protect the both of us. It got us out of there, didn't it?" But I moaned when I tasted him. That was a bell I could never unring. He heard it. He probably felt it.

"Tailor told me that if I ate someone tonight—I really did come planning to do that," I added pointedly towards Ali. *Let it go. Who cares if she thinks you're a poser?* "And he told me that if I did, he'd never trust me again. He said we couldn't be roommates. He didn't want to sleep near a predator."

Ali snorted. Ross rolled his eyes. Amber's arm lowered, and her paw was on my hip now.

"What a dick," Ross finally said after a long pause. "I woulda eaten someone like that twice."

I chuckled, and honestly Ross had a point. The only reason I'd let Tailor out now is to eat him again. In a way, Tailor was right. I had his taste, his flavor, in my mind and memory. He was delicious and filling. It scratched an itch that had come so quickly and potently. I probably would end up tossing and turning in my bed all night. While he was sleeping with one eye open, I'd be salivating at the thought of him. His lean body had felt so good going down. The fullness and heaviness in my lap felt so good. I couldn't explain it in words. It was an existential emptiness finally satisfied.

Maybe one last time, Tailor had gotten in my head. Had I changed? For the better? For the worse? Fuck it. I didn't come to a party to deal with big philosophical questions. I came to have a good time. So yeah, maybe I *was* different than I was this morning. Who cares? A lot can happen in a day. I kept going to the gym because I wasn't happy with myself and I wanted to be different. Now I was. I curled my fingers in my belly fur. Soon, Tailor would digest and become a part of the new me. I took a single resigned breath. The only sounds in the circle was the ruckus in my stomach. I couldn't pick out any of Tailor's words, though from the tone, I guessed they weren't kind. The indignant shouts were muffled by my belly. All four of us stared at my thrashing middle.

With one arm still around my waist, Amber laid her other paw on the top of my stomach's bloated dome. "If you belch out his air," she said flatly, "he'll pass out sooner. It's a common courtesy for a less willing prey."

"Ehh," Ross grunted. "I like the thrashing."

"Yeah, well Chance isn't over five hundred pounds."

"Point taken."

She pushed down, and a pressure started to build in my chest. I couldn't do anything to stop it. A rush of air went up my throat, and a wet belch exploded from my lips. Just like that, the pressure abated a bit, like when my ears would pop on an airplane. A tangier acrid version of Tailor's flavor meandered in my mouth, just under my nose. Sandalwood and bile. It felt weird and pleasant and shameful and relaxing.

"Better?"

I leaned back against the couch and nodded. The movements in my stomach had increased in energy. They started to feel spastic even, but the yelling had stopped. Sound was replaced by emphatic thunks. It was pitiful. The large curled-up-body-shaped lump in my lap was helpless to my whims. For all his struggles, it came down to me to decide how much longer this was dragged on. I felt bad for the guy. It didn't have to be this way, but he forced my paw in all of this. He thought he could control me. He thought he knew what was best for me. In the end, he couldn't even figure out what was best for himself. Inhaling deeply, I pounded my chest twice with a fist and let out the loudest longest belch I could force. "*Bwooooouuuuurrrrrrrrrrrrp!* Oof." My flesh contracted tightly around Tailor's form, displaying the shapes even more distinctly against my belly's tautness. He pawed against my stomach with a last-ditch sense of haste and urgency. Then... nothing. Just weight.

I sighed.

"How you feeling?" Amber asked. Her tone was stoic, but there was concern in her deep brown eyes.

I made a so-so motion with my paw. Emotionally I was fine. Physically I was exhausted. "Putting a lot in you takes a lot out of you."

She chuckled. "First time can be hard, but it gets easier the more you do it."

I nodded and rubbed her belly again. Bianca was still moving, but not aggressively so. Then from across the nook, Ali let out a loud crass belch as well. After a final throe of squirms, her stomach went still as well. "Alright. I want seconds. Wanna join me?" She turned to Ross.

"You bet."

"You in front."

The Orca let out a gut-shaking belly laugh. "Fair enough." Before he left, though, he looked down at me. "You have a good rest of your night. Maybe next time we do this I'll join in. I would love a chance to slip *you* down my throat. I got a thing for freshmen."

Rubbing the back of my head, I chuckled nervously. "Yeah. Sure thing." Then I paused, as the reality of those words set in. "Wait... next time?" I had tried to get chummy the last few minutes to make up for the drama, but I wasn't sure if it would work. I honestly couldn't believe these guys wanted to see me again. Either they were hard to annoy, or Ross thought I looked really delicious.

"Hell yeah. Just promise that if you bring another friend, make sure this one knows their place in the world."

Smiling, I nodded. "You got it, big guy."

"I like this kid," he said over his shoulder to Ali with a fat finger pointed right at me.

With a bashful grin, I shook my head. My ears splayed, and noticing this, Amber shouldered me. "What's that look about? Happy that *senpai* noticed you?"

"No, no," I said. "Gah it's stupid."

Ross paused mid-step, waiting for me to voice my dumb

embarrassing thoughts.

"It's just... it's nice to feel like I finally fit in somewhere is all." *God, you're such a sap, Chance.*

Ross rubbed his enormous belly. "Around here, kitten, *everyone* fits."

It was hard to tell if that was a tease, a threat, a warning, a promise, a joke, or a sentiment of acceptance. The Orca reminded me a little of Max. Maybe not being easy to read was just a predator thing I would have to get used to. With that, he lumbered back down the stairs with heavy clomping steps. Ali joined him, her tail waving daintily behind her.

"You going to go down with them too?" I asked the Hyena.

"Nah. I'm full. *Urrrrrp.*" Patting her belly created a subtle *plap plap* sound that I thought was cute. Bianca stirred, but it seemed like she still had enough air to breathe just fine.

"You two close?" I asked with a nod at her tummy.

"Oh very... now." I couldn't help but crack a grin. It was such a bad joke, that it was good. Then Amber added, "Not really. Just a few classes together. But I can feel her breathing nice and slowly. It's like when you meditate and you get that circular breathing, except it's a circle within a circle. She's not putting up a fuss, so it feels nice to keep it going. What do you say, B?" she called down to her middle with a bit of extra volume. "You doing okay in there?"

A swell nodded up and down through her furry flab.

"Okay. Kick me a few times if it starts to sting. I'll burp out the rest of your air." Another smaller swell rose up and then fell. If I interpreted it correctly, it was a thumbs up.

The smell of Amber's breath lingered in the air. When I inhaled, I could smell the faint remnants of Bianca's flavor.

"Heh. No wonder Ali likes Pigs."

"Ali *is* a pig. Only person I know who can gorge as much as she does and not gain weight."

I shrugged. Rubbing my belly, I said, "I'm starting to think that being skinny is overrated."

"You're a nice guy."

"For a pred?" I think that second guessing came from Tailor. Hopefully those little brain-worms would fade away as he digested.

"Preds can be good guys." Her smile was so sincere. Her eyes so pretty.

Fuck it. I'm going for it.

We were already practically nose to nose. I kissed her. I held my lips against her for two Mississippis. I didn't push into it. She didn't either. I just wanted to feel if there would be that zing of energy. When I pulled away, I blushed hard. Her expression softened.

"Well you sure don't waste any time," she commented with a chuckle.

"Well..." I shrugged my shoulders. "You never know when you might get eaten."

"Very fair," she agreed, and then she kissed me, and there it was. The zing. My heart pounded and I could feel her soft body lean in against me. My firm stuffed belly cradled into the softness of hers. I wrapped a paw around her pliant middle and pressed my lips into her hard. No. She was applying the pressure. Her paw cupped around my head, fingers scritching through my fur. When I kissed her, there was nothing. When she kissed me, there was passion. She was in control of it all, even whether or not the same mashing of lips made me feel something.

When she finally broke contact, I sighed. It was a rush if there ever was one, and she seemed satisfied too. She smiled, and I could see all of her gleaming fangs. It was infectious. There was something about Amber that just made me feel comfortable and at ease, even despite the fact that not ten minutes ago there was a chance she would have eaten me alive. Maybe it was because she had been so instrumental in my devouring Tailor. Her aide in pinning the Siamese Cat down had helped make it happen. "You know, I wasn't bluffing," I said leaning my forehead against hers.

"Mm?"

"When I said I'd date a predator."

She gave me one last smooch, a quick peck and then she scooted away so that she could look at me better. "Well in that case, we'll have to bulk you up more so Ross can't snatch ya up."

"Yeah," I said rubbing the back of my head. "I may abstain from the next of these games. Don't wanna tempt fate."

"Traditional hunting it is. That will make you a formidable predator."

"I'd be down for that. After all I'm gonna need a new work-out partner. I sorta ate mine."

"I'll tell ya what. I'll help you out with the Predation department if you can help me in the homework department, because *I* sorta ate my tutor." She patted her belly, and Bianca squirmed.

I chuckled. "I'm probably not the best guy to help with homework. Besides, are we even in any clas-"

"Astronomy," Amber cut in. "I always sit in the back because whiners kept complaining to the professor that my early-morning stomach grumblings made them too nervous to focus." The Hyena girl stood up and added, "Got anything going on Tuesday after class?"

I shook my head.

"Meet me in the library. If you bring that skinny Coyote who always sits in your row, we can make it a... duo-subject study session."

"It's a date."

"Sounds good." Amber got up to her feet. "I'm gonna go track down Abe. I just remembered that he drove here tonight, and while he probably won't fit in the driver's seat of his Prius anyway, I wanna make sure he's got a ride."

I nodded, smiled, and watched her leave. With no one else left in the nook, I whipped out my phone—it was actually quite difficult to reach my pocket with my gut so stuffed—so that I could enter a reminder for our date on my calendar. That was when I noticed a little message icon from Furrynook. I tapped it open and saw a new message from Max: "Hey. Still alive?"

I rolled my eyes, and I was about to respond with some

well-deserved snark, when I had a better idea. Peeling back the busted flaps of my forced-open shirt, I held my cell phone over my stomach-smothered lap, aiming the camera at my huge roommate-stuffed gut. I could only barely see the screen from how high I had to lift it to get all of my belly in the viewfinder. After snapping several photos, I picked out the least blurry one, and sent it.

He replied with a simple colon, dash, capital D emoticon, after which he then probed me for dirty details. I told him I'd tell him in the morning. For now, I just wanted to relax and revel in my accomplishment. I'd proven so many people wrong today about so many things, and I was absolutely glowing with smug self-satisfaction. It was staggering to think that, not even twelve hours ago, I'd been just outside this building worried about abs and egos.

Loud thumping footsteps drew my attention back to the stairs, and like a beast of the sea rising from beneath the waves, Ross's big black and white head lifted over the horizon of the carpeted floor. When his belly clomped into view, it bore a fresh new squirming bulge. He scratched at his tummy and sighed. "Ah. That hit the spot."

Putting my phone away, I smirked. "You finally full?"

"Eh, I suppose."

"Ali still down there?"

Ross's cheeks turned a little red and he rubbed his belly. "Not exactly."

I shook my head. "What did she *just* say not five minutes ago?"

"Yeah. She put the idea in my—*Urrrrrp!*—head. Her fault, not mine. She was scoping out for a Piggy and not paying attention. I know it's douchey to eat someone who's already eaten someone, what with how full bellies weigh you down, but to be fair, she'd only eaten a Mouse. Hardly a meal. She was on the prowl for more food, so I'd say it's fair game. Also, watching you guys play made my mouth water. I *had* to have at least *one* of you."

"I guess I should count myself lucky that Amber stayed with me."

Ross strolled over to the couch and sat down. The cushionless furniture groaned. "Eh, I saw her making googly eyes at ya. I'm not stupid enough to mess with a guy she likes. Did that once, and hoo boy, did she lay it into me. Let that be a lesson to you. Even someone with no hope to eat you can still scare the shit out of you."

"Noted."

Ross winced. "So, with Drake jerking off in his room, it was between Ali and Abe, and Abe's fucking wasted. I'm not gonna go after someone who's barely conscious. I'm not a *total* dick." He paused. "You're definitely into Amber, right? I thought I saw there might be something between you and Ali, but at the same time, it didn't seem like it."

"No, no," I said waving it off. "There's definitely nothing between us... except your belly." *Yup, that joke doesn't get old.*

Grinning, Ross said, "Good. Don't wanna alienate a potential pledge."

"It's all good, big guy."

"*Urrrrrp!* Oof. Wolf breath. Heh. Anyways, I wanted to come up and tell you job well done."

"Oh?"

"You got the hallmark of a real pred, and I think you'd make a great Gamma Upsilon Tau if you rush next year. You made the right call with eating your roommate."

"Thanks, Ross."

He nodded like it was no big deal, but the encouragement and approval really filled me with a warm fuzzy, and I didn't mean the Cat in my stomach.

"That other cat-" he pointed at my gut- "made a huge mistake tonight."

"What's that?"

"Not to fuck with chance." He let that linger, and I wondered if he was implying a double meaning. I think he might have been, and I just nodded appreciatively. "Anyways," he said after a pause, "feel free to stick around. I know the dorms make a big deal if someone eats their own roommate, but that can be this little circle's little secret. Might be a good idea to lay low for a bit in my opinion. You can help yourself to a couch if you wanna digest for a bit first. Don't worry. I won't eat you as long as you're out of my face by noon." There was a hint of jocularity in that offer, but it could be hard to tell with preds.

"Thanks."

"I'm gonna turn in. I have a lot of Anthros to churn. Have a good one, kid." He stood up, but rather than head back down the stairs, he turned right down one of the hallways of doors. As he passed me, his big Orca tail thwacked the bottle and sent it spinning for a few rotations, and when it finally stopped, the green glass neck aimed right at me. Staring down at it, I felt just a tinge of unease. After all, how does something like that *not* get interpreted as an omen? But then I just started laughing. The one time the bottle pointed at me was when it didn't count for shit.

Once Ross's heavy footsteps faded away, melting into the pulse of the loud stereo bass downstairs, it was just me and my roommate... or at least what was *left* of my roommate. Honestly, he wasn't even *that* anymore. Now he was just food. Delicious, delicious food. Meat. Prey. Game. And I won.